YOU ARE
NOT WHAT WE
EXPECTED

Also by Sidura Ludwig

Holding My Breath

YOU ARE
NOT WHAT WE
EXPECTED

SIDURA LUDWIG

Published in Canada in 2020 and the USA in 2020 by House of Anansi Press Inc.
www.houseofanansi.com

House of Anansi Press is committed to protecting our natural environment.
This book is made of material from well-managed FSC®-certified forests,
recycled materials, and other controlled sources.

24 23 22 21 20   1 2 3 4 5

Library and Archives Canada Cataloguing in Publication

Title: You are not what we expected / Sidura Ludwig.
Names: Ludwig, Sidura, author.
Description: Short stories.
Identifiers: Canadiana (print) 20190169338 | Canadiana (ebook) 20190169370
ISBN 9781487007348   (softcover) | ISBN 9781487007355 (EPUB)
ISBN 9781487007362 (Kindle)
Classification: LCC PS8623.U29 Y68 2020 | DDC C813/.6—dc23

Cover design: Jennifer Lum
Text design and typesetting: Alysia Shewchuk

Canada Council   Conseil des Arts
for the Arts   du Canada

ONTARIO ARTS COUNCIL
CONSEIL DES ARTS DE L'ONTARIO
an Ontario government agency
un organisme du gouvernement de l'Ontario

We acknowledge for their financial support of our publishing program the Canada Council for
the Arts, the Ontario Arts Council, and the Government of Canada.

Printed and bound in Canada

MIX
Paper from
responsible sources
FSC® C103567

For Jason

CONTENTS

The Flag

ISAAC WOULD LIKE PEOPLE to understand that the world has rules, and that these rules should not be ignored. You should not kill another human being. You should not steal. You should make an effort to look after your community and help it to flourish. And you should never, not under any circumstances, fly one country's flag underneath another's.

"It's degrading!" he is yelling at the man with the black velvet skullcap. "It's disrespectful! I can't even stand to look at what you've done. You want to honour Israel, but you've done just the opposite!"

The man, the principal of the very school Isaac has barged into, is nodding his head politely — albeit with his arms crossed in front of his chest, his back very straight, feet shoulder-width apart. As Isaac berates him, the principal wonders if now is the right time to organize proper security at the school. Don't ask how Isaac (elderly, short, inconspicuous) managed to just walk right into this building. Other schools in this predominately Jewish neighbourhood just north of Toronto have elaborate security checks, offices positioned right by the front door, secretaries with panic buttons, security guards out front. But Isaac was just out on his morning walk. He was just taking the route he always takes, past the brownstone townhouses, past the strip mall filled with kosher shops, a bakery, a pizza parlour. Past the Lubavitch community centre and then past the houses on the boulevard, which are starting to look tired from all the children who live in them. Tired the way a favourite T-shirt gets frayed and faded on someone who, over the years, has put on ten pounds. He walks past all the bicycles and scooters, the double strollers parked on the narrow front lawns, and then passes this school, of which he never took notice. Until today. On the flagpole there are two flags instead of one. And the Israeli flag is flying below the Canadian.

The principal takes a breath when Isaac appears to have paused. "Every year, the week of Israel's birthday, we fly the Israeli flag in its honour," he says. "Many of our graduates go on to make aliyah. We proudly support Eretz Yisroel."

"So invest in another flagpole!" Isaac yells.

"We'll take your suggestion under consideration." The principal places his hand on Isaac's shoulder, leading him to the front door.

"No you won't! You're going to ignore me. You know, there are 193 flagpoles at the United Nations. This is about international law!"

One of the teachers, a young woman in a knit beret and an ankle-length denim skirt, has stopped to watch the commotion.

"Rabbi," she says, her voice quiet but shaking, "should I call security?"

The principal shakes his head. They both know there is no security. They would have to call the police. And Isaac, while certainly irate, is hardly threatening. "The gentleman was just leaving."

"I'm still waiting for an answer!" Isaac bellows. Before today he never knew the strength of his own voice, understood the power of his words. He feels like an opera singer, a baritone reaching his climax, his mouth wide open, his hand outstretched and then clenched as he comes to his resounding conclusion. And yet he doesn't want to finish. He could argue like this all day.

"You're a caring man," the principal says, opening the door, pushing Isaac firmly but gently through the doorway to the spring air, cool against his hot face. "Really, I appreciate you bringing this to our attention."

And then, before Isaac can say any more, the door is shut. The principal locks it, making a note to send a memo to all staff that the front door must be locked at all times until further notice.

Isaac stands facing the door for a long time. Long enough to watch the principal walk back down the hall and up the stairs to his office, where Isaac knows he will ignore everything that happened during the last fifteen minutes. Isaac is standing in the shadow of the two flags. He steps away from it to be in the sun. He looks up and wonders if he couldn't just take the flag down himself. But he is in clear view of some men from the synagogue next door taking a cigarette break. And there are all the children in the classrooms. Isaac walks away panting, his heart beating so wildly the blood pounds against his ears and he feels as if his whole face is pulsating.

THAT NIGHT HE HAS supper with his landlady, Mona, a Russian seamstress who uses her living room as her workshop. They eat in front of the television. There are swatches of material draped over folding chairs, cascading down from bookshelves.

"These girls, they don't know," she is complaining. "They want to be sexy bridesmaids. But they bring me this crap material and it's going to hang on them like crap. And you know what? They will be shitty brides- maids. And I don't want no one telling no one they came to see me."

They are eating cabbage soup and pumpernickel bread. Isaac is already on his second bowl. He dumps the bread into the soup, laps up the broth, and loves

Mona for saving him from a Stouffer's microwave meal. They are watching *Jeopardy!* The topic is Chinese Geography for $500.

"Dongguan," Mona calls out, the correct answer.

"You'd have a lot of money by now," Isaac tells her. He knows the bridesmaids are not good about paying. They've been late with their deposits. They've been trying to bargain.

"I want you to make me a shirt," he says, suddenly.

Her wide-set eyes go soft. Isaac counts the wrinkles by the tops of her cheeks as she smiles.

"Oh, I could make you a nice shirt," she tells him. "Such a nice one for your broad shoulders."

ISAAC LIVES IN A basement apartment, with his own separate entrance at the side of the house. It is the darkest basement he has ever had in his seventy-two years. When he is home, he leaves the small wide-screen TV on. His younger sister, Elaine, gave the TV to him after he agreed to move back here.

"You need to get out and meet people," she said when she delivered the TV, as though the gift came with a caveat. "It's not healthy for you to stay in here all day. You're forgetting how to be with people."

Isaac leaves the TV on TSN during the afternoon and pretends he is wandering through the PGA tournament, shaking hand with Tiger Woods. The colours from the TV reflect off the floor tiles and Isaac even turns up the brightness on the screen. If it's a sunny day on the course, he will put his face to the TV and feel the heat from the electricity, like the California sun, burning his nose. Isaac has lived many places — seven countries out of the 193 whose flags each occupy a pole at the United Nations. Of all of them, Israel was the most beautiful. There he was on kibbutz in 1969, turning the desert into fertile farmland. His arms were a Sabra brown. His forehead blistered from the heat. When he showered at the end of the day, the water ran brown off his body, as brown as the roads they were paving in Tel Aviv. Brown, he once thought, was the true colour of renewal, the beginning of a seed, the colour of potential. All of Israel was brown then, and he could fade happily into the landscape.

But now here? In Thornhill, north of Toronto? Isaac sees a lot of white. Even when it isn't winter, he sees clean white pavement, white stucco houses, pale white people translucent in the spring as they emerge from their hibernation. Forget multiculturalism; Canada is the whitest country he has ever known, as if nothing ever changes.

ISAAC LEAVES HIS HOME only after it has gone dark outside. He sees Mona through the living room window. She is sleeping in front of the news, which is reporting the Canadian Armed Forces have lost another soldier in Kandahar. Her mouth hangs open while a woman, about her age, weeps on the TV screen for her son who died. The ticker at the bottom describes her as "grieving mother."

"There's a man who would know better than to hang a country's flag below another," Isaac mutters. There's a man who knows about respecting world freedom.

In the night, the neighbourhood glows beneath the street lamps, white light streaming onto the pavement. There is a lilac bush near the curb that sparkles beneath this spotlight. Other people are out too. They wear spring jackets and look down as they walk. Isaac passes a religious woman and wishes her a good evening, but she doesn't look up. He is not wearing a jacket and he does not feel the cold. When he tries to greet someone else who passes him and is once again ignored, Isaac thinks, *Yes, I am invisible.*

The two flags are still up. He stands beneath the pole and pins a skullcap to his head, black velvet, the one he keeps in his sock drawer to take with him whenever he visits the religious couple two blocks over for a Friday night meal. He met them once at the kosher Sobeys, standing in the checkout line. They want to move to Israel someday. They could hardly believe he left it. *They will like this story*, he thinks as he reaches up for the cords and pulls. *They would do the same thing if they would just look up and notice.*

Nobody stops him as he stands there on private school grounds, lowering the flags and unhooking the

Israeli one from its rope. Maybe that's the trick to thievery, to make the act into an illusion. Isaac pretends he is a caretaker removing the flag as has been requested of him. He stands the way a caretaker might stand at the end of a long day, his shoulders a bit stooped. He even takes a break to arch his back, which is not at all aching. Once he removes the flag, Isaac folds it up and carries it back home like a gift, a blue-and-white-striped gift he will present to his landlady and say, *Here. Make me a shirt with this. Let me pay you double.*

Now this is material, Mona might respond. *You are a man with good taste.*

"IT'S NYLON!" SHE EXCLAIMS the next morning. "How am I supposed to sew with this?"

"I don't know," he tells her. "With a needle and thread?"

"You trying to be Israeli? You think you are a Sabra?"

"I think that this will make a good shirt."

She looks at him through her squint. She says, "You pay me double."

THE SHIRT HANGS HEAVILY on Isaac's shoulders. He sweats as he walks in it. The cuffs feel like weights around his wrists. But the people who pass see him now, the blazing Star of David on his back. In this neighbourhood they give him the thumbs-up. Two religious teenaged boys with knit *kippahs* yell, *"Am Yisrael Chai!"*

from across the street. Isaac waves to everyone. "Mona made this," he tells them, though no one knows or cares who Mona is.

And then Isaac reaches the school. It's 10 a.m. and the preschool children are out for recess. Isaac stands by a chain-link fence, hands on his hips, the two blue stripes of the flag stretching across his chest, wavy over his shoulders, over the bump of his protruding belly. He turns around so that the back of the shirt is facing the playground and he feels the wind gusting down the back of his neck, blowing the shirt outwards from his body like a balloon — no, a sail on a Zionistic ship leading the proud boat to the shores of Haifa. He hears a child behind him running to the fence, the clanging of the metal like the bells on that ship, and then the horn as it docks.

"You're wearing a flag!" the boy says. Isaac has not turned back around. He's waiting for the sound of others coming, the pounding of feet against the pavement when they all turn to see. If he were really a boat, the shrieks of wonder at his arrival.

"My auntie lives in Israel." The boy keeps talking. "I have a flag in my room. And a stuffed camel with a flag for the saddle."

There is screeching, but it's not directed at Isaac. Just the sounds of kids playing tag, of four-year-olds arguing over whose turn it is to go down the slide. Giggles from hide-and-seek inside a wide plastic tunnel. And then he hears a woman calling, "Yaakov! Don't stand by the fence! Come over here to play!"

The fence dings again. Isaac turns around and the boy is running away, the tassels from his *tzitzit* hanging out from under his shirt and flapping in the wind. Isaac remembers the men and the boys who wore those in Israel, those anti-State, freeloading, they-don't-even-pay-taxes-but-they-use-the-state-of-the-art-hospitals-for-the-births-of-their-thirteen-children, no-good religious Jews. Isaac is now holding on to the fence. He's now shaking the metal links with all his strength. He's spitting while he yells, "That's right! Run away! All of you! Run from what really matters!"

And now heads are turning. Now the teacher who called away little Yaakov is holding the boy as if Isaac might come crashing through that fence any minute. She's the same teacher who asked the principal about calling security when Isaac was last in the building. Today she's wearing runners beneath her denim skirt, but the skirt is so long she would trip if she had to run at full speed, if she had to gather all these children and race them inside to protect their pious heads.

Isaac is about to yell something at her. Something about the baselessness of God, the stupidity of Jews like her who teach children to save the world by holing themselves up in dingy classrooms and studying ancient texts that are no more than fairy tales! And then he sees the front door of the school swing open, as easily as it opened the other day when he barged inside. Out comes the principal, his black velvet *kippah* askew from moving so quickly. He probably ran down the stairs from the staff room when he heard the commotion. He probably wished he could fly out the window when he heard Isaac was back.

"Hey!" the principal calls, as Isaac turns his back again and starts running. Isaac spreads his arms out as he leaves the property, running up the street toward the Lubavitch centre, the kosher strip mall. He feels the wind again, streaming down his back, and this time he really is that ship, the flag puffed out as a sail pushing his aging frame faster, farther than he thought he could go. He hears the principal's footsteps pounding closer and he laughs. Right now he feels like he will never stop.

Pufferman

PUFFER'S MOTHER BUYS caramel-flavoured rice cakes. She's told Dayle, the nanny, that Puffer can have as many rice cakes as he wants. But Dayle buys Lay's salt and vinegar chips at the Mac's Milk on the corner of Bathurst and Atkinson. She keeps them in a plastic storage bin under her bed in her room in the basement. She lets Puffer sit on her bed with his pack of untouched rice cakes and they eat the chips together watching *Days of Our Lives*. *Days* finishes ten minutes before Puffer's mum comes home from the gym. It's enough time for Puffer to wash his face and hands, brush his teeth, and then eat two of the caramel rice cakes so that when she kisses him, that's what she smells. He even crumbles one in his hand and then runs his fingers through his hair so that she will smell the salted caramel as soon as she hugs him. He does this in Dayle's bathroom, shaking the crumbs out of his hair over her sink. She says it's alright. This way he won't tell on her for watching *Days*.

Dayle rinses out the sink while Puffer runs up the stairs to say hi to his mum, who has never asked about why the water is always running when she comes home.

Puffer's dad does not want to pay for Dayle anymore, but Puffer's mum insists that Dayle is non-negotiable now that she has to raise two boys on her own. So the lawyers have argued over Dayle for weeks. In the meantime, Puffer floats in his backyard pool, his bloated stomach, his puffed-out arms like a floaty toy thrown into the water and forgotten. Puffer's mother talks on the phone in the kitchen with the window open. Puffer can hear her. She's saying she will have to look for work. *Something in marketing. His tart. Like he wanted to get caught. I have a business degree, you know.*

Dayle sits on the green woven recliner, but she is not reclining. Dayle is hunched over her phone. The rice cakes and water are on the white plastic side table. Under the chair, in the shade, hidden from Puffer's mum, who will come out soon to say she's heading out, there is a pink Tupperware bowl full of Cheezies. When Puffer comes out of the pool, he will sit on the other side of the table, on the matching recliner, and he will eat those Cheezies until his fingers glow orange, coating his lips. He will stick out his bright tongue to get Dayle's attention. Orange like a disease. He'll say, "It's da plague! Ahhh!" Or leprosy. Or something new like Puffer Face. He'll say, "Dayle, I'm contagious!"

And she'll say, "Stay away from me. I can't bring disease back to my country!"

Dayle is heading home soon to the Philippines for a vacation. She takes the threat of disease very seriously. While Puffer splashes around in the pool, Dayle stares at her smartphone where she is trying to Skype with her children. Her call keeps getting cut off. When she finally gives up, she tells Puffer to come out of the pool so she can show him the pictures her mother just texted through of her son, seven years old, wearing Puffer's old Roots T-shirt. Dayle is allowed to take anything of Puffer's that no longer fits him. And, of course, he goes through clothes fast because Puffer is Puffer. He climbs out of the pool and wraps his towel around his shoulders. It's too small to wrap around his body. Instead, it's like the cape of an overweight superhero. Pufferman. Dayle hands him the bowl of Cheezies and says, "Finish this."

When he was born, his parents called him Sean. But even then he was a fat baby. His brother, Jared, three years older, would pinch his bloated arms and call him Puffer, like some yellow toy duck that he could squeeze to make bubbles in the bath water. The nickname stuck. In the last year, it has been as if Puffer was attached to a helium machine. He has a face like a blowfish: round cheeks, inflated, pushing against his nostrils, puckering his lips. He wheezes when he breathes because of partially obstructed airways. He whistles when he blows air out of his mouth. That's the sound he makes running to first at baseball, the air coming out of his kissy-face mouth in a high-pitched squeal, like a train in the distance, but never getting close enough to roar.

The cuffs on his baseball jersey sleeves cut into his arms, which are spongy like hotdog buns. His stomach pulls on the fabric so that his team logo, a lion, gets all scrunched together when he sits down on the bench. The lion's mouth closes; the eyes bunch up like they're winking. It's as if he's folded that king of the jungle into an alley cat. Sometimes Puffer feels like the monster at the top of the food chain. The big toothy goon that swallows everything below it whole.

His underwear wedges up his bum when he's out on the field with his baseball team, waiting to catch a fly ball. Puffer's dad does baseball. That's part of the agreement. Jared is away with his best friend, Adam, at sleepover camp, so it's just Dad and Puff on baseball nights. The team plays in the field beside the Jewish school that's going to be torn down for townhouses. Puffer went to that school for a couple of years before his dad pulled him out because the tuition was bleeding him dry. And what was the point spending a half-day in class learning a language he was never going to use? When Puffer is up to bat, he thinks about smashing the ball sideways so that it sails up to one of the windows on the top floor, shatters the glass all over a teacher's desk like a bomb. Like the first one to start tearing the place down. He fouls every ball when trying and strikes out. His underwear is stuck up the crack of his bum and he tugs at his shorts before sitting back down on the bench.

In the car, on the way home, after the Lions have lost again, his dad says, "What's with that weird dance you were doing out there, Puff?"

Puffer shrugs, "Wedgies."

"Your undies too small? You telling me your mum can't be arsed to buy you new undies?"

Puffer blows air into his cheeks, wheezes it out slowly through his nose. His dad says *arsed* because these days he's into watching gritty British crime dramas on Netflix. Puffer could have walked home from the field, but his dad brought the car and accompanying Puffer back to the house is part of the agreement. Puffer looks out the window at the back of the golf course where the chain-link fence meets the sidewalk up the hill. There are faded flyers and coffee cups along the boulevard. Blown up against the fence is an open, empty pizza box. Puffer says, "I'm hungry."

His dad says, "Lazy bitch," and he grips the steering wheel while Puffer whistles through his teeth.

"Don't," his dad says.

"What? I'm breathing."

"Breathe quietly like the rest of us."

Puffer's dad couldn't be arsed to hide his cellphone a year ago when Puffer took it off the kitchen table to play *Subway Surfers*. That's when the text came through of that woman's boobs. Two weeks later, when his parents sat him and Jared down to talk divorce, they started by giving them both their own iPads. Their mum even said they could take them to school the next day.

"I got a divorce present!" Puffer told his friends, who crowded around him at recess to take turns on *Minecraft*. His throat hurt when he said it, and when the bell rang and everyone ran away, Puffer felt like he was underwater, like everyone was floating around him but he couldn't hear them properly because of the current. They were floating out of his reach.

In the two minutes it takes to get from the field to the house, Puffer's father hits the steering wheel with his palm five times.

"What the hell am I paying her for if she's still dressing you in last year's clothes? How many new shirts did she buy for herself last week? Eh? How about shoes?"

Puffer wheezes like he's running uphill, even though he's not moving a muscle. He feels his cheeks going red-hot. His tongue becomes heavy and dry. His dad keeps asking questions and he can't answer any of them.

"How about her nails, eh Puff? She still keeping that appointment every Wednesday? Or the gym? She still seeing that trainer? The hell . . . am I paying for her to be some Barbie doll for some asshole investment banker?"

Puffer gets out of the car in the driveway and he can't swallow because of his sore throat. His dad gets out, slams his door, and runs up the steps by twos. He's pounding on the front door while Puffer stays on the bottom step, turns his back to look up at the sky, the power lines down the hill leading toward the 407 highway, the sound of the electricity constantly buzzing, which Puffer has never noticed until now, when he's looking for something, anything, else to focus on. He clenches his teeth and he breathes loudly to match the pitch of the electricity. It works. Behind him, his parents are having a brutal screaming match, but right there on the walkway, Puffer generates enough energy in his breathing to burn up each and every word his parents lob at each other. Puffer is an iPad game, zapping those insults as they hover above his head—*sorry excuse for ... asshole ... my lawyer will ... fuck you ... and you ... and you ...*

DAYLE HAS TAKEN ALL of Puffer's shirts. She has laid them on his bed, folded neatly, arms tucked behind. When Puffer comes into his room, she looks up and says, "Your mum order you the new clothes from Old Navy. Tell her you need the underwear."

Dayle has also taken out Puffer's underwear. It looks so small when it's piled one on top of the other like that. Puffer says, "Dayle, that's gross."

Dayle says, "I wash them. With bleach."

Puffer climbs on his bed and crawls under his covers. Dayle tells him to take a shower, but Puffer puts his head under his pillow. Downstairs he can hear his mother crying on the phone... *the HELL he thinks... humiliates me... I'M the mother... Make us move...* Puffer tucks the ends of the pillow around his ears so that all he hears is his heart beating inside his head, or is it the sound of his arteries pumping the blood away from his face? Because that's how he feels now, cold face, light-headed, like a wind howling inside him, a single, whistling wind on an empty street.

JARED AND HIS FRIEND Adam went to camp for the whole summer. Adam lives with his grandmother and used to hang out with Jared at the Promenade Mall cinema, until he got caught stealing coins from the arcades. Adam said that his grandmother was sending him to camp because "the bitch doesn't want me getting arrested." His sister, Ava, plays on Puffer's baseball team. She's the only runner slower than Puff. Puffer knows Ava is keeping him from being a total and complete loser, and he likes her for that. But no, he is not going to invite her over to swim like his mother used to bug him to do. She used to say, "Be nice to her. Some kids have it a lot harder than you do." That is, until Dad and the boobs lady. Mum hasn't mentioned Ava since.

Puffer is sitting on one of the loungers by the pool with a camp letter from Jared. It says: *Tell Mum Adam and I were nearly eaten by a bear. Seriously. Tell her a bear ate away at my arm and I'm using a branch as a prosthesis. Tell her I'm carrying a stump with my one hand in case the bear comes back again and gets at one of my legs. Tell her it's like a freaking horror show here. They let the bears run wild.*

"Hey, Dayle," Puffer says. They are sitting out by the pool again. Dayle wears oversized sunglasses. Puffer's legs are turning red, like the neck of a smoked pig. Dayle looks up from her phone and Puffer says, "He was eaten by a bear."

Dayle doesn't laugh. She says, "No bear would eat your brother. Too sour."

But Puffer is still laughing. He's thinking of what his mum will say when he tells her. He's already embellishing the story in his head — *The camp wrote to me. It was his dying wish. The other counsellors watched him being devoured and he begged them — tell my little brother that I love him! Tell him that he's awesome. Pufferman's my superhero.*

Dayle stands up. She raises her phone toward the sky like a metal detector and she turns around, like there is a beam somewhere she's trying to catch. She says, "The Wi-Fi sucks out here." When she's rotated twice with nothing, she turns to Puffer and says, "You wait here for me."

But Puffer is hardly listening. He's working on the bear story that grows bigger and bigger in his imagination. He's thinking about something to do with hitchhiking. All good horror stories start with hitchhiking. His brother in his lumberjack shirt and his cargo shorts, his thumb stuck out near the highway because he's running away from camp. He's trying to come home to spend the summer with Puffer by the pool, the two of them making up bear stories about their parents. *She falls into the bear's den at the zoo. The bear eats everything but her fingers because of the chemicals from her manicure.*

Puffer can hear Dayle in the kitchen on her smartphone, talking quickly in Tagalog. Puffer doesn't know any Tagalog, but he can tell she's arguing with her husband. Probably something about their kid, how she's sacrificing everything to give him the best chance in life. *Do you want to switch places? Do you want to come babysit this overweight, whistling boy? You tell your son to come talk to his mother. You tell him how much I'm doing.*

Puffer stands up to go back in the water. He jumps off the diving board and sinks to the bottom of the pool. He watches for Dayle's wavy shadow when she comes racing out to see what's happened to him, listens for her frantic call, the lilt in her voice like a doorbell—*Puff...* *Er?* His chest begins to hurt, and he hears the blood whooshing by his ears. There's a whistle in that too, like a leak in a valve, like a trickle of something being left behind. Puffer closes his eyes because they are starting to sting, and he's trying hard not to float up. He fills his cheeks with air and then swallows it back in sips. But that does nothing to quell the panic in his chest, that feeling that he will never be found and no one will care. It's like he's one of those stupid blowfish shrinking so that he can lie on the bottom of the ocean completely undetected until he chooses to puff out. That element of spikey surprise.

And then there's a whoosh, a current of water pushing against him, a tiny hand grabbing him by the elbow, rushing him up from the underneath. His eyes are still closed when they break the surface of the water, but Puffer can't help his mouth opening, the way his lungs expand and contract as he gasps for air. The sound of him sobbing like a million balloons deflating.

"You try to kill me?" Dayle's saying. She's yelling. She is also gasping for air in big, heavy gulps. "You try to get me fired?"

But she doesn't leave him. She leads him to the shallow end, where they stand together up against the wall. Puffer slips an elbow up onto the deck, lays his heavy head on his arms, and cries while Dayle rubs his back. She tells him, "You big boy now. Okay? No more hide-and-seek. You always tell me where you are."

You Are Not
What We Expected

RINA LOOKED OVER AT her husband, Shalom, sitting on the couch beside his mother. He wouldn't look up. He fingered the fringes of his *tzitzit*, wrapping them around his forefinger until the skin on the tip turned purple. His name meant *peace,* as well as *hello* and *goodbye.* Rina thought, *He's never known whether he is coming or going.*

"I have nowhere to go," Rina whispered. She heard how foreign she sounded, had always sounded, since moving into this suburban home in Thornhill four years ago, into this family that had been Canadian for three generations. When she moved here from Melbourne, she brought containers of Milo chocolate powder, Vegemite, and *R*s that make the ends of her words sound as if they are left open, unfinished. *Cah* instead of *car. Weh* instead of *where.*

"You can stay in your suite. We would never leave you homeless," the mother-in-law continued. She held

Shalom's hand, as if this was hard for him to say. Except he said nothing. Rina realized that the couch cushion he was sitting on had a chocolate handprint hidden on the underside. She had turned it a few weeks back after their eighteen-month-old daughter, Sarah, had got into the mother-in-law's chocolates.

"Shalom will move back into his room," the mother-in-law said. "You can stay until you find your feet. Of course, Sarah will be looked after. But you are not what we expected."

. . .

THE MORNING AFTER HER mother-in-law delivered the separation, Rina could not stop shaking. When she arrived to drop Sarah at the home daycare before her shift, Bryna said, "You look really pale. Are you alright?"

Bryna had six children of her own and was ten years older than Rina. As Bryna reached for Sarah, three toddlers behind her started fighting over a riding toy in the living room, which had been blocked off by a pet gate. One leaned over to bite the girl who was currently holding the handlebar of the plastic bike made to look like a police motorcycle. The house smelled like Pine-Sol and sour milk. Rina backed away as Sarah started crying. Before she could answer, Bryna had already closed the front door, was scolding the biting child loudly enough that Rina could still hear her.

"In this house, we share!"

RINA WAS STILL SHAKING during her shift at the kosher Second Cup and she spilled the hot chocolate on her hand. When she yelped, Priscilla turned from the cash, said, "Run it under cold water before you blister."

Rina rinsed her hand under the water and waved to Priscilla, who *tsked*. Priscilla was from the Philippines and doing courses at night to update her nursing qualifications. She'd been on a constant climb since entering the country and first living in someone's dank basement, folding their laundry, making chicken cutlets and steamed vegetables for their kids for dinner. On her breaks, Priscilla read from her textbooks and wrote practice exams. She'd told Rina, "My husband and kids will come next year. We will finally be together."

Rina took deep breaths and held a paper cup under the hot chocolate machine. An elderly man with a tremor, a regular customer, had ordered it and was waiting in one of the plush seats. She added cold milk to cool the drink down and she felt a pinch in her throat at never having thought to do that before. Priscilla would have. She was good at thinking ahead. Rina wouldn't look at her shift mate. If she did, she might not be able to stop herself from screaming at the sensation of falling while Priscilla kept moving higher.

RINA'S MOTHER-IN-LAW had long argued for them to hire a live-in nanny for Sarah.

"You could go back to school," she'd presented to Rina. "And the girl could also clean while the baby sleeps. Your shifts would cover the cost. You aren't paying rent."

These were the signs Rina had not considered until now.

How she'd argued that night in the basement with Shalom, who, of course, took his mother's side. "They are very generous. This would be a way for us to give back."

"We need to save for our own place!"

"Then you need to help out more upstairs. She notices that. She says you hide out down here and you never let her be with the baby."

It's because I don't want to be erased! Rina wanted to yell, but didn't.

How she felt a tingling in her fingers when she watched her mother-in-law holding the baby, cooing at her, "Who's Bubby's girl?"

How her mother-in-law would turn her back to Rina so that Sarah wouldn't reach for her. It didn't take long for the baby to be distracted by the mother-in-law's chunky silver bracelets, her long, beaded necklaces. And the mother-in-law would say to Rina without turning around, "You can leave us alone. We're good."

That tingling in her fingers, in her toes, crawling up her flesh, made Rina feel as if she were disintegrating without Sarah. Because of course they were good without her. She'd known for a long time that if she walked out of the house right then, no one would try to chase her down. Her mother-in-law would have stood at the window with Sarah, waving.

AT NIGHT, RINA LET Sarah fall asleep next to her. Sarah had dried banana in her hair from lunch. Rina had made a mental note to bathe her in the morning, but the thought was as fleeting as a daydream, as concrete as her plan to call a taxi, grab her daughter, and run to the airport. Her sister in Israel had been texting her all day. Even now, her phone buzzed on the floor beside her bed.

You have rights.

You tell Shalom my husband knows lawyers.

Reen? Where are you? Why won't you answer?

Rina's sister was named Simi. Her husband called her by her first syllable, Sim. As in *simply.* Simply wonderful. Simply beautiful. They had five children and they lived in an apartment in Modi'in where they shared Shabbat dinners and lunches with friends in their building. Simply joyous. Simi covered her hair with tie-dyed scarves and wore long, dangling earrings. She had her Ph.D. in genetics. Three years ago, Rina had been nineteen, on a gap year in Israel at seminary, dreaming of her sister's life. When she brought Shalom to meet them, he told a joke about Moses and Jesus playing golf and everyone laughed. Afterwards, Simi said, "He fits right in."

Now, Rina lay next to Sarah and listened to Shalom and her in-laws stepping back and forth across the main floor. Her mother-in-law's voice was shrill, loud enough that Rina could hear when she was speaking, but not enough that she could make out the words. Just the tone, high-pitched and overbearing—the one she used when offering excuses. *She talks back to me. And you see how she hides the girl. Shalom, that baby doesn't even look like you. I can't have a daughter-in-law who makes me a fool.* She couldn't hear if Shalom was responding. He was so soft-spoken. Rina used to say he centred her.

Now she closed her eyes and said the *Shema* before going to sleep. *Hear O Israel, the Lord Our God, the Lord Is One.* She was floating in this dark space, saying words she didn't believe anyone else would hear. This wasn't a commandment. It was a plea. *Please hear me. Please don't let me fall away.*

THE NEXT MORNING, Rina's shift started at ten. She mixed Sarah's cereal with some applesauce and scattered a handful of Cheerios on her high-chair tray. Upstairs, doors opened and closed. The chime of the alarm system. Someone stamped as they put on their boots. The mother-in-law called out to the father-in-law about something he was supposed to bring home from the office. The squeal of the automatic garage door, the levers and pulleys stretching and grinding to carry the door up. Rina listened for Shalom's soft steps coming toward the basement door. She kept expecting him to come down the stairs, walking lightly on his toes, his finger to his lips, his other arm outstretched toward her. Tucked in his pocket would be three plane tickets to Israel.

You see, he would say, without even having to speak, *I have been saving all this time.*

Sarah banged on the tray and her Cheerios jumped like crickets. She laughed and banged again. Rina put her finger to her lips to shush her, but Sarah flapped her hands in front of her face and shook her head no. And then Rina realized that everyone upstairs had left. Even Shalom, getting a ride with his father to the subway station rather than taking the bus. Rather than at least coming down to say good morning to Sarah, or even to figure out the day. *Would you pick her up at daycare? What time is dinner? Would you give her a bath tonight? I was too tired last night to do it. I had a really bad day. Maybe we could have some time tonight, just the two of us? I'm feeling so closed in.* Rina kept looking at the stairs while Sarah shrieked for her attention. Sarah seemed to understand. *Hey, Mum, remember that separation? Guess what? It starts now.*

RINA DROPPED SARAH AT Bryna's and remembered to go to the side door and not the front. When she signed

Sarah up, Bryna told her no parking on other people's driveway, and don't come in and out the front door where everyone can see. *I don't need the neighbours calling me out.* The houses on Esther Crescent were built so close together, Rina could touch the wall of Bryna's neighbour while waiting for Bryna to open the side door. There were already twenty kids playing in the basement. A tower of blocks fell. Someone had a croupy cough.

Bryna's teenaged sister opened the door. "Sarah! Are you ready to do painting today? And songs at lunch-time? She's so cute. She loves when we play 'Bum, Bum A-Rolly.' Has she shown you?"

Rina peeked inside and saw Bryna changing a diaper on the floor. Another adult downstairs told two girls to share nicely with the dolls. Rina did the division in her head, the adult-to-child ratio, and like every morning concluded that it's the loving home environment that counts. She said, "I may be late today, alright? You'll tell Bryna?"

"Aw-righ," the girl imitated, but not cruelly. She sighed, "You have the coolest accent."

RINA LEARNED FROM HER MISTAKES. Today she was being extra careful with the hot chocolate. The man with the tremor was back and his wife had ordered him the drink before settling him into one of the plush armchairs while she went to Sobeys to do her shopping.

After paying Rina for the drink, she handed her a tip, placed it in the palm of her hand, the one that Rina had burned the day before. The woman said, "For yesterday. I know all this isn't easy."

Rina's mouth went dry. Did she know? Did everybody know? Was this crazy, insular neighbourhood so inward-looking it could see right through her?

"Your hand," the woman said. "Oscar was so concerned. People don't appreciate the risks in this kind of work, do they? Anyway, treat yourself. Later today. From the two of us."

There was a tip jar on the counter, but the woman motioned for Rina to put the money in her pocket, a twenty-dollar bill. Priscilla wasn't looking up, her head bent over her textbook, her hand holding her hair off her face so that it stuck out around her head like a crown. Rina thought, *Priscilla, Queen of the Night School.*

As she carried the drink over to the man, Rina was thinking about skipping the Shabbat circle time tomorrow at the Promenade Mall drop-in centre. She didn't think she could sit amongst the other mums, the nannies, the woman at the keyboard with her frosted big blond hair, her thick Russian-Israeli accent and her mix of Hebrew and English. "Okay, *yeladim! Mee rotzeh* to be sleeping bunny?" She felt like putting Sarah in her stroller, taking the subway somewhere far away from here, walking in one of those downtown neighbourhoods that the morning radio host described as *bustling.*

Was there a shooting in one of them last week? Rina couldn't be sure. Parkdale, the Danforth, the Annex. The names all blended together for her as places other people went to. But now, left in the basement as she was, Rina had the sudden thought: Was she other people?

As Rina set the hot chocolate down on the coffee table in front of him, Oscar put his trembling hand on her arm and applied pressure as he stood. She lost her balance, and with his other hand, he steadied her shoulder. For that moment, they were supporting each other.

"Bathroom," he whispered. The word came out wet, some spit dribbling out of the side of his mouth. Rina recoiled; the dribble and the request made her think of the man peeing.

"It's right there. Around the corner," she told him, backing away. He leaned toward her, his arm outstretched as if they were attached. His face was unevenly shaven, like his uneven speech.

"The corner?" he managed. Rina nodded and pointed. He smelled like dry mouth. His grey eyes widened as if he were afraid of everything around them.

"I'll save your spot for you," she promised him, even though the café was almost empty. "Take as long as you need."

Priscilla looked up, frowning. The man manoeuvred himself around the furniture, dragging his right leg behind him, gripping the backs of chairs, and then the wall. Priscilla stood up and walked over to offer him

her elbow. He pushed her away, perhaps unintention-
ally, but Priscilla stepped back and turned toward Rina,
pointing. "He wanted you to help."

Rina's phone pinged. A WhatsApp from Simi. *You
have to do something.*

She was about to tell Priscilla to mind her own
business when the man turned the corner toward the
bathroom, wobbled, and then fell forward. He called
out "Elaine!" as he went down. His head and torso
smacked against the doorframe, the sink, and the bang-
ing sounded like the entire café was crumbling. Rina's
mouth was still open, prepared to lash out at Priscilla,
but instead she said, "Call for help!"

Blood pooled on the ground by the man's head. His
mouth was twisted and one eye squeezed shut, as if he
didn't want to see. But then the other was wide open,
as if he couldn't help himself. He couldn't help himself.
Rina didn't know where to look. She didn't know how
to breathe. In the background she could hear Priscilla
yelling on the phone, "Yes! An ambulance! Don't you
understand me?"

The man moved his open eye to Rina's face and she
knelt down toward his lips, which were moving. His
breath came out shallow and fast. He reminded her of
a fish on the floor of a boat, begging to be thrown back
in the water.

"You're not alone," she told him. "I won't leave you."
And yet, even as she said it, she heard the hollowness

of that empty promise. She would leave him. As soon as the paramedics arrived, she would bolt up from her spot on the floor as if to tag them in a sick game of relay. She would move past Oscar's wife, who would be standing near the front door, her bags of groceries scattered over the floor, the red sauce from the prepared chicken leaking everywhere.

"You are not alone," she whispered again, but she knew the words were barely audible. She could barely hear them herself. She held the man's hand and she counted in her head until she could hear the siren in the distance. Either the siren or maybe Sarah calling for her. Wailing.

"We're almost there," she said, this time a little louder. She squeezed the man's hand and he seemed to breathe slower. Rina too. Pretty soon she'd be able to leave. Someone swung open the front door. There was yelling and chairs scraping across the floor. Pretty soon she'd have no reason left to stay.

The Elaine Levine Club

ISAAC EATS A CEREAL called Harvest Fibre Plus, the one that comes with dried blueberries that taste like jellybeans trying to have blueberry flavour. The taste is so sharp it settles beneath his nose. If he were to eat a handful of those so-called blueberries he would get nauseous. But sprinkled amongst his bran flakes and maple oat clusters, it's just enough of a treat to feel like he's cheating at breakfast.

Isaac has a bowel movement before 8:30 a.m. every morning. That's how he knows the cereal is working. Everything in moderation.

Since he moved back to Toronto, his sister Elaine has offered to do him little favours here and there. She's smart. He knows what she's up to, looking after him so that he'll stay. She calls him in the morning and she says, "I'm doing a Costco run. Do you want me to pick you up any of that cereal you like?"

He has plenty already. There are three unopened boxes in his closet because Sobeys had it on sale last week. But still, he'll say, "Sure. Pick me up a box." In L.A. no one ever called offering to do him a favour. Elaine doesn't frame it in this way. She tells him, "I'll give you the box tonight when you come to watch the kids." She's weighing him down here in boxes of organic flakes and he doesn't even care.

ELAINE IS MEETING HER doppelgängers tonight. Her Elaine Levine Club—a bunch of senior women who like to get together because they happen to have the same name. When Isaac comes into the house, he smells his sister's rose perfume. Their mother used to wear a similar scent when she would go out on a Saturday night. Isaac is dizzy from the memory of her sitting at her vanity, the scent lingering around her like a cloud and floating slowly toward him as he stood in the bedroom doorway. As Elaine now rushes down the stairs, Isaac sees his mother, her scent billowing behind her legs like a wave, reaching for her stole over the banister. He blinks and she's gone. It's just Elaine waving at him as she applies her lipstick in front of the hall mirror. She purses her lips together and then relaxes them into a smile, leans in to check her teeth.

"I made the kids one of those pizzas. There's enough for all three of you. Don't let Adam have any more Halloween candy. He has trouble sleeping."

Isaac says, "I thought grandparents were supposed to let their grandkids eat all the junk?"

Elaine eyes Isaac's reflection in the mirror. She looks so much like their mother did—eyebrow raised when Isaac went too far, which was always; wide nostrils that made her appear more handsome than pretty. Isaac never noticed a mother-daughter resemblance with Elaine's estranged daughter, Carly. Perhaps that's not a coincidence.

"How did you find this group again?" he asks.

"Facebook. They're nice women. We've been messaging."

"Clubs are for hobbies. What could you possibly all have in common?"

"I like the company." She throws on a blue scarf with embroidered flowers that match her lipstick. The colours flash like blinking lights as she turns toward the door. "I won't be late. Make sure the kids are in bed by nine. Maybe Adam won't fight if it's you."

Isaac snorts. He takes off his shoes and heads for the newspaper still folded on the kitchen table. That's another thing—Elaine won't get rid of her subscription because she knows Isaac comes over every day to read it.

"I won't be late!" she calls again, the grandchildren not responding but playing video games in the family room. Isaac settles down to read about world traged-ies, a couple of tourists gone missing in Mexico, a mass shooting in Texas and not everyone accounted for, a child kidnapped somewhere in Ohio. *All these people missing*, he thinks. *Maybe they just don't want to be found.*

AT 9:15 P.M., ISAAC LOOKS UP and realizes that the kids haven't moved. He can't remember being so still at that age. Adam is eleven, cross-legged on the floor in basketball shorts and a T-shirt for the Toronto Blue Jays. He's playing some military game on the TV with headphones. There are silent explosions everywhere. Ava, nine, lies on the couch with an iPhone close to her face, watching some sitcom. Isaac thinks about all the wannabe actors in L.A. coffee shops, the ones chasing careers on the big screen, and how everything boils down to this — a performance that can fit in the palm of your hand. If entertainment is supposed to be an escape, how can anyone get lost in a dream that small?

"Hey," he says, and then clears his throat. "Hey! Your grandmother said for you to get ready for bed now."

Ava doesn't look up. Adam definitely doesn't hear him. Isaac says "Hey!" a little louder and Ava mumbles, "Just a minute. It's almost done."

When he was little, Isaac never contradicted authority or tried to bargain. He certainly was never allowed to just sit there when an adult was speaking to him. You got up when an adult entered the room. You said, "Yes, sir." You put your book away. (That's right! Whatever happened to good old-fashioned reading?) And you were in bed by eight, lights out. Your mother made sure you had a good night's sleep. Isaac can't decide whether to rip the electronics out of their hands and tell them just how spoiled, entitled, and doomed their generation is, or whether to afford them some sympathy. Because when he was a kid he knew of no one whose mother dumped them with their grandmother and then took off.

"Assholes," Isaac says out loud, though he doesn't realize it. Only when Ava and Adam look over at him and Ava says, "Did you just swear?" Adam starts laughing, even with the headphones on.

"He did! He totally did," Adam says, too loudly because of the explosions in his ears. Isaac wonders if the Wi-Fi in the house is somehow connected to his thoughts. Is Adam hearing everything through those blasted headphones?

"That's right, assholes!" Isaac says. Now he's smiling too, as if he's cracked the code for getting this generation to listen. "I said bedtime!"

AFTER THE KIDS WASH UP, Adam calls down. "Uncle Isaac?"

Elaine's couch sags in the middle, so that's where Isaac sits, in the dip just the right depth and circumference for his behind. He's closed his eyes and is meditating on not being pissed off at his sister for tricking him into babysitting for the price of a jumbo box of cereal.

He can't even work her goddamn TV because Adam's always got it hooked up to that Xbox/Wii-thing. *X*, indeed. When he was little, *X* stood for nothing. That nothing box.

"Isaac?"

"Yeah?"

"Can you come here?"

"I don't know," Isaac mumbles. His legs are half asleep. It will take three tries before he can swing himself out of this couch hole. He was going to just sit here until Elaine came home, fall asleep, maybe wave her away when she tries to wake him and instead accept the blanket she tucks in around him, settling fully once all the lights click off.

Isaac leans forward for momentum, but Adam is now standing in front of him. He's still dressed in the shorts and T-shirt. He needs a haircut. His brown hair is thick and sticking out in tufts around his head. If he were a girl, he would be wearing it in long waves down his shoulders. People would be envious of his hair.

"Uncle Isaac," Adam says, this time whispering because he's right there in front of him. Elaine's mentioned how worried she is that he doesn't sleep. ADHD, anxiety. Well, is it any wonder? Isaac reads in the paper all the time about how to set up kids for success. Structure, rules, responsibility. Nothing about pity, that's for sure.

Adam says, "When are you going back?"

"Going back where?"

"To L.A. Isn't it sunny there, all the time?"

"Yeah. It's nice. It's hot. It's not like here, I tell you."

Adam shifts his weight back and forth from leg to leg, like a downhill skier. He'd make a good athlete, Isaac thinks. All skinny like that. All muscle.

"I wanna move there. When I'm older," Adam says. "I wanna be a gamer. Or, like, an action actor. Or maybe a stunt man. I can do stunts. Awesome stunts."

"Sure you can," Isaac says. Now he wants Elaine home this minute. Now everything about this house feels stuffy and closed in. Everything about this Toronto suburb, built in the boring, safe eighties, when no one took risks. *I was travelling the world*, Isaac thinks, *while Elaine and Oscar were buying this house off the builder's plans.* Who wants to be in the same place for thirty years? *Stale*, that's the word. Elaine begged him to come here and it's like she's served him stale food. His mouth feels pasty. He says, "You're supposed to be in bed."

"I don't feel like it."

"Tough. You're not allowed to be out of bed."

"I can't lie still."

And Isaac gets that. The hardest thing about moving here is the feeling that everyone is lying still because there's nowhere else to go.

THE NEXT MORNING, Isaac walks to Sobeys. He's had an issue with Sobeys since he moved here. There's a

sign on the side of the grocery store that claims it is
the largest kosher supermarket in North America. In
North America! This was the basis of one of his first
arguments with Elaine:

"That's impossible. I lived in L.A. Pico Boulevard
has kosher grocery stores five times the size of Sobeys!
And in New York. You've never been to some of those
suburbs. They make Thornhill look like a quaint town.
They have kosher bakeries bigger than Sobeys. Liquor
stores!" By the time he was picturing all the alcohol,
Isaac was roaring. As if he were preparing to lead an
army of kosher wine bottles into the Sobeys to protest.
Elaine shook her head, which Isaac took as an argument. But really, she just didn't care. She said, "So take
it up with head office. I'm sure they have their statistics
to back it up."

"It's simple square footage! You don't need statistics. You just do the math! How big is the space? And
if it's not bigger than the largest kosher grocery store
in L.A., then your marketing is false. And there are
standards in place to deal with that. False advertising.
This community should be up in arms that they are
being lied to and they are falling for it and *paying* for it
every time they walk into that store and buy a package
of overpriced chicken."

Elaine was making a said "overpriced" chicken for
supper. She was rinsing the pieces under cold water
while Isaac spoke with such passion that he spit out

the word *priced*. She said, "Isaac, of all the issues in the world. Really?"

ISAAC STRIDES ACROSS THE Sobeys parking lot and prepares himself to demand a meeting with the store manager. He wants to know the exact square footage of the store. He enters armed with that information from the largest kosher grocery store in L.A. When he called them, they were happy to give it to him over the phone. In fact, the manager was shocked to hear that a store in Canada was claiming to be larger.

"*Be'emet?*" said the Israeli-sounding man. "There are that many kosher Jews up there? I don't believe it."

"Neither do I," Isaac mumbles as he marches into Sobeys. Oh, he promised that store manager a full report. They spoke for forty-five minutes. That was a man who understood customer service! He said, "You come visit me when you're back in town. I make the best schnitzel in L.A. Freshest. You'll have lunch on me."

Isaac's mouth watered at the thought. He could start a class-action lawsuit with the pending information. Overpriced food supplementing false claims. And the community pays for it! He would use his take from the results of the suit to finance his trip back. He would say to Elaine, after the legal proceedings were all over, "What did I tell you? You don't need me here anymore. You and your Elaines can thank me for saving you hundreds of dollars a year in groceries!"

He walks up to the customer service desk and he announces, "I'm here to see the manager."

The woman behind the desk, Asian, small, is helping another customer buy a lottery ticket. The customer is an elderly woman dressed in a heavy fur coat with a blue knit hat. Her white hair sticks out from below it in tufts like dandelion seeds on the verge of being blown away. The customer looks over at Isaac and says, "Wait your turn."

Isaac spots a Russian accent. He says, "*Nyet, nyet.* This isn't communist Russia! She can call the manager while she sells you your sorry excuse for life savings. This woman is smart enough to do two things at once."

The clerk looks up at Isaac. "I'll help you in a minute."

Isaac yells to no one in particular, "How hard is it to get service when you're preparing a lawsuit?"

The power in that word. He's convinced even the music through the store speakers (1960s forgotten hits) halts at his proclamation. A man with a white-and-green badge on the lapel of his suit jacket comes over and stands behind the counter. He crosses his arms. Isaac knows body language. The crossed arms. Feet shoulder-width apart. Chest puffed out and face frozen. The man says, "What are you looking for?"

Isaac points at the manager, leaning on the counter. He says, "What is the square footage of this store?" He's salivating from the excitement of his pending free lunch. He smells roses and lilies from the florist counter next to customer service. And stale coffee from the machine offering a cup for a loonie. It's the scent of victory. He doesn't need the caffeine. Isaac is buzzing with righteous indignation.

"I'm not authorized to provide you with that information," the manager says.

"I'm not asking for something top secret. You have a store here. It's a certain size. You have hundreds of customers every day walking these aisles. So what do you say, fifteen thousand square feet? Twenty?"

Isaac has done this before, demanded information, watched his target grow pale with nerves. Isaac is not a tall man. The manager is much taller than he is. Isaac is stout. Round. His glasses are always foggy and Elaine bugs him to clean the lenses. But Isaac sees everything clearly — the manager's Adam's apple bobbing at his throat as he swallows, stalling for time; the Asian woman frozen beside him, unable to predict what Isaac will do next. When he lived in Australia, he once got an audience with the postmaster general over the unfair distribution of collectible stamps. In New York, it was with the manager of the bar that Woody Allen liked to frequent. They were claiming to sell Glenfiddich, but Isaac can taste a J&B from just one sip. They all responded to him, every time. The customer is always right.

"You are committing false advertising," Isaac continues. He shakes his finger at the manager's face.

"There is no way this is the largest kosher grocery store in North America. No way! Haven't you been to L.A.? New York? Their kosher communities would eat yours for breakfast. But you know you can tell the Jews of Thornhill anything and they will believe the almighty Sobeys. Well, you can't fool me! And I won't allow this kind of deception to continue!" His voice rises on *deception*. With his peripheral vision he can see the heads turning. The truth unfolding and all these shoppers, their minds blown.

The manager says, "If you have an issue with our advertising, you will have to take that up with head office and the marketing department. Those decisions are made at that level. I can assure you that our store provides a service to this community that is not matched anywhere else—"

"Stale bread!" Isaac yells. "Rotten prepared food! This is not a service. This is a food-safety catastrophe waiting to happen! It's a wonder you haven't been shut down by the city. Your store is the laughing stock of all the other grocery stores in a five-kilometre radius."

"You need to leave now," the manager says.

"You cannot keep me quiet. I will fight for customer rights! We have a right to fair and honest advertising—"

"You need to leave or I will call the police."

Isaac has also been here before. When they threaten with the police, it usually means they have nothing in their artillery to argue back. He sees this as a sign that he has won and leaves willingly. Isaac does not need to be dragged out of a kosher grocery store. He knows everyone is watching him. The silence is so obvious as he leaves, it reminds him of resounding applause.

"AIN'T THAT THE TRUTH," Isaac mutters. He detests daytime television, but Dr. Phil is telling it to him like it is.

"You've got to pull yourself together. You have responsibilities. It's time now to grow up and take control of your life. Because you matter to other people. Now, I know you don't believe me. And we're gonna get you some help so that you can start to understand these messages I'm telling you. But you do matter. And this self-destructive behaviour, well, it just has to stop."

All the time the camera is on the woman whose face is streaked with tears as she hiccups back her sobs. Isaac had turned on the TV hoping for the baseball game, while waiting for the Sobeys marketing department to call. They will be checking their facts and then ringing him up with an apology. Perhaps a token for his troubles. He might even refer the customer service rep who calls to Dr. Phil by saying, "You know, no one gets ahead by ignoring the truth."

Isaac used to have a therapist who sounded like Dr. Phil. Back in L.A. A man with a soft Southern drawl who said stuff like "You have to think of your mind as not something that controls you, but as something that you can control. So turn it off when it's too loud. You're the one with the finger on that switch."

His therapist had the relaxed manner of someone who drank tap beer. Isaac didn't drink beer, but he trusted a man who did. His therapist was shorter than Dr. Phil, and he never mentioned God (thank God for that), but he was bald. At their last session together, Isaac noted how the sun came in through the window and hit the shiny skin across his scalp, not like a halo but like the marking of a hole where a beam of light might one day come shooting out and upward. The therapist said, "I believe that change is good. This move. I think you'll find the change of scenery will give you a change of perspective."

"I won't stay there long," Isaac told him. He said it like a promise. His therapist looked at his watch and then folded his hands. He replied, "I wouldn't put a time limit on it if I were you."

ISAAC'S HOME PHONE RINGS before he can switch the channel to baseball.

"Right on time," he mutters, taking in a deep breath, pulling back his shoulders.

"Hello," he answers, fully expecting the manager of customer service to say, "Isaac. Thank you for bringing this to our attention."

But instead it's Elaine, breathless.

"Isaac? She's yelling at me all over Facebook. How does that happen?"

"Who?"

"Carly. She's blaming me for not telling her about Oscar. She's been AWOL for almost two years, and now it's my fault?"

Isaac tucks his portable phone between his ear and his shoulder. He turns his back on the commercial for Pop-Tarts, which are exploding over the screen in cartoon strawberry jam. He reaches for his laptop computer. He says, "Hold on, let me see here." He can feel his sister's panic like a clothes dryer cycling up, the high-pitched whirl of a spin that will tumble everything until it blends together and the sum is indistinguishable from the parts. He has cycled like that before. Years ago it took his own mother months before she sent him a letter telling him his father had died. Isaac was in Singapore. The letter started, *I would have told you sooner, but I didn't know where you were.* For sure he wanted to blast her for that. He would have sent a tsunami over the ocean, if he could have, just so his mother could be soaked with a fraction of his grief.

When the Facebook window finally loads, Carly's post is right there at the top of his feed. *Go to hell, Elaine Levine! You are dead to me. What kind of mother doesn't tell her own daughter that her father died? There is a special place in hell for people like you.*

Below the post some friends have answered with: *???*; *Are you alright, hon?*; *I'm here if you need me*; *Sorry for your loss.*

And then, below them all, an Elaine Levine who is not Isaac's sister writes, *You've tagged the wrong Elaine. Please remove this tag.*

Elaine says to Isaac, "I haven't even told the Elaines about Carly. She's too much to explain. They're all coming over to me tomorrow. I was going to tell them soon, but now I guess I don't have a choice."

Carly's tagged Isaac too. He can see his name in blue even though she doesn't mention him in her venom. But it's like a jab or a bump in the ribs. *I see you too,* she's saying. *Don't think for a second that I don't.*

"Yeah, Lainy," he says, closing the screen. Dr. Phil's baritone is still in the background. Isaac feels an adapted Southern twang on his tongue when he says, "The truth is out."

ISAAC GOES OVER TO Elaine's the next day when he knows the kids will be at school. She's usually out—Elaine and her learning projects. A tech course for seniors at the Beth Tikvah congregation. Mah-jong. Her shift in the kitchen at that centre for adults with developmental disabilities. Elaine blasted him recently when he used the word *retarded*. There had been a group of those kids at the pizza place learning how to order lunch. He said to her how nice it was that these retarded kids could learn important life skills. She told him she would hang up the phone if he ever used that term again.

"You of all people should understand how important it is not to label."

Isaac took issue with that. He of all people. But she'd moved the conversation on before he could ask her what label she would slap on him.

He's thinking about Elaine's Tim Hortons coffee and maybe a slice of that chocolate loaf she buys from the Israeli bakery in between his place and hers. He's hoping the Sobeys office will try his cellphone when they decide to reach him. He gave them both numbers, home and cell. He's imagining the call coming in. How his phone will display the caller so he can be prepared before he answers.

When he rounds the corner and sees all the cars in front of Elaine's house, he's so lost in his fantasy that he has forgotten what she said about her doppelgänger club meeting today. There are at least five cars parked on the driveway and by the curb. For a minute he is overtaken by clothes-dryer panic that she's enlisted an army of people to help her push him out.

He opens the front door with the flourish of someone arriving to stop a pending disaster.

"Elaine!" he calls out before he's even taken in the scene before him.

Seven women turn at the sound of their name. They freeze as if Isaac has pressed the Pause button on a remote, tea mugs to lips, hands stopped midway from rubbing off crumbs. There is that chocolate flaky loaf he loves on the dining room table in front of them. Coffee already made. He steps back into a relaxed stance because Elaine, his sister, is using their mother's good cocoa set, which means she's not planning to go anywhere. Not with all the washing-up to come.

"This must be Isaac," one of them says.

"Yes," his sister answers. "My brother. Isaac, this is the Elaine Levine Club. I thought I told you they would be here today."

"Well," he says loudly. Affronted. "I guess that's not the first time you forgot to mention something important."

His sister's face goes from white to pink, like a wine spill crawling up her neck and across her cheeks. She says to her group, "As you can see, my daughter, Carly, isn't the only one in the family who can be difficult to love."

The other women look nothing like his sister. They seem to vary in age anywhere from fifty to seventy years old. Although truth be told, he was never good at guessing women's ages. One reminds him of his mother's old friend from Trinidad, short frizzy hair, skin like creamy coffee, a splatter of freckles up and down her arms and across her soft, wide cheeks. The last time he saw her was at his mother's funeral. She said, *You should have been nicer to your mother. All your gallivanting.*

"Some people can be," that Elaine says, while the others nod as if washing their support all over Isaac's sister. Waves and waves with every tilt of their chins.

"So what?" he says out loud, although the women aren't paying attention to him anymore. What did that mean anyway? Easy to love. He walks into the kitchen with Dr. Phil in his head, saying, "Love's not supposed to be easy. No one said you get a free ride with love."

He pours himself a cup of coffee and ignores the newspaper waiting for him on the table. Instead, he moves to the doorway of the living room, where the women have now moved on to talking about something else. Carly already forgotten. He says, "You know, chances are, none of you are easy to love."

They stop talking to look over at him with mouths open, ready to rebut but at a loss for words. He is about to continue to deliver his sister's message about not applying labels to people (how would she like that!) when his phone rings. The ring tone sounds like a 1980s desktop phone, a bell so loud you could hear it from anywhere in the house. The digital display shows SOBEYS NA INC, and he holds up the phone to show Elaine, nodding his head, pointing. *You see? This is what happens when you dismiss me.* Isaac taps to accept the call. He is fully aware of all the silence around him when he says, "Yes, I'm here."

Escape Routes

IT'S BEEN SO LONG NOW that Ava has to pause before she remembers Kovi's name. Even though for one summer he was her best friend, and even though she almost killed him. But she has no problem remembering the smell of the garbage. That was the summer of the strike in York Region, so shiny black bags piled up on the hot pavement, leaned against each other like tired old men, like her grandfather propped up on the couch but also slouched over because of his weak right side. That was the summer Ava and her brother, Adam, moved in with their grandparents, waiting for their mother to figure stuff out. When Ava sat next to her grandfather on the couch, she smelled his sour breath. But then, it was no better outside. Outside, she'd breathe in the scent of rotten scraps from last night's dinner, forgotten fruit from the corners of the neighbourhood refrigerators, soft bruised apples, shrivelled lemons, bananas so ripe they folded into their brown selves and leaked out of those garbage bags all over the pavement. Ava has willfully forgotten Kovi because he left, didn't he. Eventually the garbage got all cleaned up, and Kovi with it.

Ava was eight years old when she rode around on her mother's old bicycle, candy apple red with rust in the corners and joints like copper shadows. There used to be streamers hanging from the handlebars, but they'd almost all fallen off. All but one string on each handle, drooping like Kovi's mother's thin braid that hung down the middle of her back until right above her bum, the end shaped like a fingernail, pointing. Ava used baby oil to keep her pedals from squeaking, and so even amongst the stench of the garbage, when she would ride to Kovi's apartment building, her feet smelled like baby. Like the top of Kovi's baby sister's head.

"Here," Kovi said, when Ava arrived. He leaned over to sniff the baby, sleeping in her mother's arms in the rocking chair. Ava leaned over too and she caught it, that sweet, perfect scent shielded from the rot outside. Kovi's mother said something to him in Russian. Kovi said, "Your grandmother, she knows where you are?"

Ava shrugged her shoulders. How far could she get on her bicycle anyway? They didn't know where her mother had run to. Everything was relative.

THAT SUMMER, Ava's ten-year-old brother, Adam, stayed inside and played video games on the Wii all day. Ava believed he was afraid of the wasps and that's why he didn't come out. She felt brave riding around on her bike, even though she kept her mouth shut, her lips clamped together in case a wasp might fly in and sting her throat. Her brother said that could happen. He didn't even take his eyes off the TV when he said it. Ava thought she was so much braver than he was, and yet, she believed everything he said.

Ava and Adam's grandfather, Oscar, used to sell office furniture, until the Parkinson's made it so that he couldn't even shave himself. Every room in their grandparents' house had a rolly chair that spun around. There were desks tucked into corners — one in the living room where Ava's grandmother sorted the mail, one in the family room for piles of magazines. The only room that didn't fit the pattern was the kitchen, where there was a large L-shaped desk that they used as their kitchen table.

Before Ava's grandfather took sick and Carly took off, there were plans to renovate the kitchen. Elaine had wanted an island. Having an island in your kitchen meant you had a large, loving family that came together on Friday nights and holidays for dinners so extensive they had to be served buffet. Elaine never gave up hope that her daughter would return, act sane, and that the whole family would all come to her for brisket on Rosh Hashana. That she would end her evening wiping the gravy stains off the granite counter; the creamed cheese and lox platter already in the fridge under Saran Wrap for the next day's lunch, when they would be back together.

Even at eight years old, Ava was learning the dangers of holding on to goals you had no control over. Her grandmother gave up her kitchen set long before she should have. She probably gave away the table and chairs to a family like Kovi's — Russian-Israeli immigrants escaping to their third attempt at an easier life by landing in Toronto. But then Oscar suddenly faced an early retirement. And when it was clear the renovation was off, he brought home the L-shaped desk with two guys from the warehouse to put it together. The children had to sit with their knees sideways on the one side because of the wood panelling to the floor on the other. Their grandfather, the former king of office furniture, sat on the inside, leaning over his soup. He dripped soup down his stubbly chin. Elaine sat beside him and wiped him up, every drip. She had been his secretary at the company, so every part of her life was about filling in his gaps, before and after he was retired. He didn't actually retire — the company retired him. And Elaine had to give his speech at his office goodbye party because even by then, the Parkinson's made him mumble. His chin quivered, as if the words he wanted to say were being mixed in a blender before he could spit them out. Like when he spat out his soup. Elaine would catch each word and rephrase before he made a mess of whatever was flowing from his mouth.

KOVI HAD AN UNCLE back in Israel who was a magician. He also sold sunglasses on a boardwalk by the beach. Before they moved to Canada, Kovi spent his summers helping his uncle with the sunglasses, and then learning card tricks. In his bedroom, he showed Ava pictures of him and his uncle wearing big, dark glasses, straw hats with brims that made half-moon shadows on their faces, people crowding around their table and Kovi standing on a folding chair with his arms out wide, as if about to gather the whole crowd for a hug. There was something about his confidence and control that made Ava wonder, *If I stood above the crowd like that, would anyone notice?*

"My uncle got on *Israel's Got Talent*. He was semifinalist!" Kovi looked for a deck of cards to show her the trick that got his uncle that far. But he could only find part of a deck. On the back of the cards was a picture of the Rocky Mountains. Ava knew from the world atlas on her grandparents' bookshelf that the Rockies descended from Alberta all the way down to New Mexico. She knew this from tracking her mother's escape route with her finger across that map: Toronto to Las Vegas, where she went to be a hairdresser for beautiful people. Ava skimmed over those mountains like stepping over a sidewalk crack (don't break your mother's back).

Ava thought Kovi's room was stuffy; the air was thicker than outside. The walls were cream-coloured with black smudges from when they moved in the furniture. He had a bunk bed and a desk they got from a cousin who had already been here for five years and had now moved into a house. A small black bookcase with sagging shelves held Hebrew books piled on top of English picture books. There was a magic kit that came in a tin box. It had metal rings that linked together and came apart without any break. Kovi knew how to do that trick, but he wouldn't show Ava.

He said, "My uncle's going to try for *America's Got Talent*. If you win, you go to Las Vegas."

"My mum's in Las Vegas!"

"They could meet!"

"Yeah!"

They were sitting on his floor and Ava's legs tingled from falling asleep. The magic rings lay between them, separate. Right then, Ava believed that Las Vegas existed only so that her mother and Kovi's uncle could fulfill their dreams and find each other and then their way back to Thornhill. Full circle.

Kovi said, "If he goes, my father says we will visit."

Ava said, "Me too!" Like it was something her grandparents had already planned. "We'll fly together!"

Kovi picked up the rings and hit them together so that they linked. "If he gets audition, he says I can be assistant. He will make me disappear."

Then he said, "Poof!" and spread his fingers so that the rings clattered to the floor.

KOVI'S MOTHER'S NAME WAS ELENA. His father was Michael and they called the new baby Nicole because Elena wanted something Canadian. Sometimes Ava stayed for dinner. Elena made oven fries and fish sticks. Or homemade pizza. If Michael was home and not on a shift, then she made chicken schnitzel and the whole apartment smelled like burnt garlic powder and hot oil. At home, Ava's grandmother made her take a shower before bed. But Ava would close the bathroom door and just run the water, sitting on the toilet while the bathroom steamed up like a cloud. Then she would come out in her pyjamas with a towel wrapped around her head. She would fall asleep with her arm across her nose, breathing in the leftover scent from Kovi's place. Her grandmother's house smelled like puréed soups—usually split pea and potato leek. And artificial citrus, because her grandmother was always disinfecting the door handles.

Her grandmother and their neighbour, Mrs. Gilani, complained about the stench as they watered their front lawns.

"I can't even bring Oscar out in this," her grandmother said. "Migraines. His tremors. My house is filled with air purifiers."

"It's unsanitary!" Mrs. Gilani said. She had long black hair down to her waist that she wore back in a silver clip with etched designs, like a spider web. Ava drew with chalk on the driveway while they spoke, each standing on her own property. She drew pictures of giant sunflowers with faces, with wide, oversized smiles. Mrs. Gilani's flowers were much prettier than Elaine's, and it made Ava mad that her grandmother couldn't grow anything beautiful. Mrs. Gilani grew impatiens and lilacs and orange tiger lilies that never seemed to shrivel up and die, leaving grey single stems. She had little wire figurines hidden in her garden — two frogs, a cat with glass eyes, and a rooster with its head cocked upward and beak wide open toward the sky. For years, Mrs. Gilani was awarded a City of Vaughan Garden of Distinction award. And still Elaine would stand out there with her hose, a nozzle with all these different ways of spraying water — mist, shower, straight, flat — and she would water the Japanese maple that she always complained wasn't growing quiet right, and the petunias that wilted every afternoon.

"It's the stench," she said. "It's killing my garden."

"It is," Mrs. Gilani agreed. Although Ava knew that couldn't be it, because Mrs. Gilani's garden was fine. She must have been lying, or withholding a magic trick, a special potion she added to her water. Ava got onto her bike to ride over to Kovi's, smudging her sunflower face.

Her grandmother called, "Be back before supper! They don't need to feed you all the time."

Ava didn't reply, but she heard Mrs. Gilani say, "You shouldn't let her play over there. With all the garbage, that building will be filled with bugs."

WHEN MICHAEL WAS HOME for supper, he told stories about his buddies in Israel. One friend had to settle up with a guy who sold cellphones. The guy wasn't paying his supplier. Michael knew the supplier. Michael was not a tall man, but he was broad. When he told this story, he held baby Nicole in one hand like a football, ate his schnitzel with the other. She curled over his shoulder and his hand was so big it covered her entire back when his fingers were spread. Her little feet shifted in her pink velvet sleeper. She mewed like a cat when he said, "Kovi, that guy. He don't listen. In Israel no one listens. They just look. They see big man with big knuckles and they think, 'You know. I like my face.' And that's how we got him to pay. Because he was afraid of my hands."

Kovi laughed and so did Ava. Kovi looked like his dad—round and wide like a wrestler. They both had a front tooth that overlapped the other, like crossed fingers behind your back when you're breaking a promise.

Elena said something in Russian and Michael responded, "What? They need to know how good they have it here! You see, Ava? Air raid sirens. Rockets. That's no way to live, right? That's no way for a boy to grow up."

Then, finishing the last bite of his schnitzel, he reached over and cupped the back of Kovi's head, pulled him in to kiss his forehead. He said to Ava, "You see? People complain all over about garbage. Who cares about garbage! You get used to it. People get used to lots of things."

Elena said, "Ava, want more?"

She always asked. Ava always said "Yes, please."

Then Michael said, "You see? We come here. New country, new home. We even have a new daughter! Right, Ava?"

He was referring to Nicole, but Ava let herself believe otherwise.

AVA'S BROTHER, ADAM, played *Wii Sports* on the TV in the family room all summer instead of playing real sports outside. The house sounded like a packed stadium, but staticky, like a car radio in a tunnel. Ava saw a lot of Adam's back that summer, his white neck, his thin shoulder blades twitching through his pyjama shirt when he swung to hit at a digital tennis ball, or when he was pounding a virtual opponent in boxing, smacking and smacking and smacking at his face.

Oscar sat in that room in the afternoons, when his tremors were worse and he was tired from his body shaking out of his control. He had a recliner chair in the corner where he slept with his head drooped toward his chest, his bottom lip hanging open, the skin on it wrinkled and cracked. On the table beside him was a glass of water with a straw, and his container of pills, divided evenly by the days of the week.

Adam grunted when he played. Sometimes he got sweaty. Ava asked if she could have a turn when his match finished. He turned around. His eyes were red from not blinking. He had a blue stain on the front of his shirt from his Gatorade. She wished she hadn't asked him. He looked like an animal she'd startled awake. Their grandfather snorted behind them in his sleep and Adam laughed.

"No," he said. And then, "Fuck off."

Ava said, "You're not supposed to swear."

He looked over at Oscar and then back at Ava. He said it louder, "Fuck off, Ava. Fuck. Off!" He was hissing. They were not supposed to wake their grandfather. If they startled him, he would cry out. He would have no control. Elaine would have to come running. She would yell at them: *I can't do this anymore! I can't take care of all of you!*

Ava held her breath and didn't move. Adam inched closer to Oscar, tiptoeing and then crouching down so that his lips were close to his ear.

Ava whispered, "Don't."

He looked over at her and smiled, but it didn't reach his eyes. He said, "Then get out."

THE ONLY TIME AVA watched TV the whole summer was at Kovi's when he had reruns of *The Fresh Prince of Bel-Air* on and they shared his couch, watching this black guy from Philadelphia figure out how to live in a posh California neighbourhood. Kovi liked the guy who played the cousin, the one who danced around to Tom Jones. Kovi took a spoon and mimicked the scene, swinging his arms so that he looked like a monkey, bobbing his head like Ava's grandfather at the end of the day when nothing was under his control. But with Kovi, Ava laughed. She cheered him on, telling him to dance again and again.

Later, from her bedroom and the open window, Ava heard her grandmother and Mrs. Gilani outside, sitting in the backyard. Mrs. Gilani smoked cigarettes, and because they were right outside the window, the scent overpowered the garbage — the mix of smoke with a hint of mint. Ava lay in bed with her mouth open, her tongue stuck out as if she could catch the scent as it blew through the window screen and then settled in her room.

Mrs. Gilani said, "You are not a nurse. We think we are nurses and teachers and accountants, but we're not."

"The wait-list at Baycrest is ridiculous," Elaine said.

"There are other places."

"I can't right now. The kids."

"And mother and chauffeur and cook. Teach them. They'll step up."

"They're younger than you realize," Elaine answered.

Ava had heard her say something like that earlier, when she was on the phone to her brother, Isaac, in L.A. They were talking about Ava's mother, Carly. Elaine said to him, "She's younger than you realize." Ava stood next to the kitchen doorway, her back against the wall so that her grandmother wouldn't see her. She had become an expert at walking through the house without making a sound. Perhaps invisibility was her magic trick. Isaac was talking a lot. Her grandmother kept starting words but missing the chance to interrupt. "Bu... Is..." It reminded Ava of jump rope, understanding the rhythm of when to leap in.

Elaine finally snapped, "I'm not asking for your opinion, Isaac. I'm telling you that she's like a child and she needs our help. You call me if you see her."

She hung up the phone while Ava slid away from the kitchen, imagining herself melting into the wall, disappearing through the cracks of this house, becoming nothing heavier than a deep sigh.

KOVI DIDN'T THINK THE garbage was disgusting. He told Ava the bins behind his building were the best places to collect bits to make his magic potions. He read the Harry Potter books in Hebrew, which he got out of the library on the other side of the mall. The library had sections for books in Hebrew, Russian,

Farsi, Mandarin. Kovi told Ava he heard people speaking Hebrew all over the place here. Thornhill was full of Israelis. In the winter, he knew he was in Canada because of the cold and snow. But in the summer, he said, Thornhill was just like Netanya but without the sea.

"I'm making a potion that can make you invisible," he said.

Ava balanced on the cement parking blocks. She pointed her toes like a gymnast.

"Me?"

"Whatever. You, me. If you want."

"You could make me disappear?"

"It's a spell," he said. "You would come back."

More than anything, Ava wanted out. Even if just for a moment. Even if she knew he would never be able to do it. She loved him right then just for trying.

They went back to Ava's house later with a full plastic grocery bag. He said, "Some ingredients I had to use other things instead. Because we don't have dragon toenails. I found chicken bones! My mother come get me after supper. Okay?"

Oscar came around the corner from the family room and waved. The TV was full of bells—short, staccato smacks. Adam shouting out, "Yes!"

Ava said, "Papa, this is my friend, Kovi."

Oscar smiled crooked. His mouth curled up high on one end so that his left eye squinted. The right side of his mouth stayed drooping. Then he went to climb the stairs, his shaking arm gripping the banister, his head leaning against the wall for more support. He took each step two feet at a time. It was going to take him forever to climb the stairs and Ava and Kovi just stood there watching. Somehow Ava knew that his body and her family were breaking down at the same rate.

Elaine was in the kitchen with her back to them, standing at the sink. The steam from the water fogged the window and blurred her reflection. Ava knew there was a lot Elaine didn't see, even when she thought she was watching them all the time. Like right then, Adam coming around the corner to use the bathroom, the game still blaring. Adam saying, "What are you guys doing?"

And Ava saying, "Kovi's making me a potion."

Adam: "Yeah?"

Kovi: "Yeah! From Harry Potter."

Ava: "I'm going to disappear."

Adam looking back at the TV. Looking forward at the bathroom. Looking back at Elaine, and then up while Oscar climbed a mountain to his bedroom. Adam saying, "Cool. I'll help."

Of course they let him help. The kids ran down to the basement, laughing and tripping over legs that couldn't move fast enough. Elaine shut off the water. Kovi squealed. He said, "This is like dungeon!"

Elaine yelled down, "Be quiet! Your grandfather's going to sleep!"

Adam looked up and raised his middle finger. He whispered, "Fuck off, you bat!"

Kovi and Ava looked at each other, mouths open, completely still. When Elaine didn't answer, they all covered their mouths and laughed into their hands. And then Adam reached into his pocket and pulled out one of Oscar's blue pills. He held it in his palm like the beginning of a magic trick. It was here. And now it's gone. He said, "Okay. So let's make this."

The basement was unfinished. It had a bathroom, but the walls and the door were just plain wood. The bathroom was the last thing Oscar did before his hand started shaking and it was no longer safe for him to hold a hammer. The toilet was pink, and so was the pedestal sink. There was a matching fuzzy bathmat between the toilet and the sink so that you didn't have to stand on the concrete floor when you were peeing or washing your hands. The rest of the basement was dark concrete. It smelled like wet cardboard and the mouldy decomposition of sewage that had nowhere else to go.

Adam stood at the sink with the bathroom door open. Kovi and Ava stayed on the couch that was folded out into a hide-a-bed, but without sheets. Sometimes Adam slept in the basement when it was too hot for him upstairs and Elaine wouldn't put on the air conditioner in case Oscar caught a chill. Adam had drawn on the walls, stick men fighting with stick guns and their little stick hearts getting blown to pieces. There were dead guys all over the walls and Ava realized that yes, this was like a dungeon, full of dead people they had forgotten about.

Kovi whined beside her. "I thought I was doing this."

"Shh," Ava said. "Adam's in grade five."

Adam had Kovi's bag of stuff. He mixed everything in a plastic margarine tub in the sink. He crushed the chicken bones with Oscar's hammer and then licked off the marrow. He jumped up and down like one of his Wii boxing players before a fight. He curled his hands into fists while he was thinking.

Kovi said, "We're moving. We found our house."

He said it like it was something they'd lost and had been looking for all this time. Ava felt her stomach ache. She wondered when she would be able to say, *I found my mum.*

But she said, "Where?"

Kovi said, "Aurora. It's called semi-detached. I get to share a pool. You can come swim!"

Aurora sounded far away. Like a star. Like a constellation. An aura. Like something you see when you shut your eyes tight and your head is pounding from heat and garbage stench and your grandmother always telling you to be quiet, like she wants you to pretend you're not there.

"It's far?" Ava asked.

He shrugged. But she could tell he'd already been. It must have been a long car ride. Once he moved, he wouldn't be coming back here. He'd be disappearing. Ava would be riding around the neighbourhood, circling his apartment building like the wasps hovering over the garbage no one would take away. And he'd be the invisible one.

Ava said, "Adam, you almost done?"

Adam used Oscar's hammer to tap the blue pill until it crushed into a soft power on the edge of the sink. He wiped it with his finger into the margarine container and it fell like snow. Snow felt like ages away. Like another world, where Kovi would have a yard and snowmen and nothing to even remember who Ava was. Like her mother, cutting beautiful people's hair, those stars with hair so blond it fell like fine white powder by her feet. Ava wondered if the sun in Las Vegas shone bright, like an aura.

Adam brought over the container. He said, "You need to drink the whole thing. Right, Harry?" He called Kovi "Harry" to make him feel a part of it all. Like it was all his idea in the first place.

Adam said, "You tell her, Harry. You tell her how if she drinks this, she'll disappear and she can go wherever she wants."

Ava looked over at Kovi and he was back to smiling. Adam knew what to say. Kovi sat up straighter on the couch. He clutched his book and shook it for emphasis. He said, "Yah! You will! You'll be like ghost. You will haunt people!"

All of the sudden, Ava couldn't stand his bright, wide eyes, his bright enthusiasm. The whole idea that just because he got to leave, that somehow she should disappear and then reappear to find him gone. "So you do it," she said to Kovi.

"Yah! Okay!" he said, but then Adam looked unsure. There was Kovi reaching out his pudgy, thick hands for the margarine container, Adam holding it steady, looking over at Ava. Adam saying, "But, Ava, I made this for you."

Ava said, "Kovi's the one who does magic. His uncle's going to be on *America's Got Talent*. Let him try."

Adam looked down at the concoction, stuck his fingers into the liquid as if to scoop out whatever powder from the pill hadn't dissolved. He lifted his hand back out and shook the drops off, saying, "Fine, whatever. This was your guys' stupid idea."

"No!" Kovi said. It came out like a bark. He leapt off the couch and grabbed the container from Adam. The liquid pooled together like an oil puddle on the pavement behind his building.

"It's not stupid idea! It's real," Kovi said. Then he gulped the whole thing down without even making a face. It smelled worse than the garbage outside. It smelled like juice from rotten fruit and old cooked meat. Aurora sounded like a place where garbage wouldn't even be allowed.

"Shit," Adam whispered. He looked at the stairs and

then back at Kovi, who was now lying on the hide-a-bed, staring upward at the ceiling, a trickle of potion running out of the corner of his mouth as he said, "It's working. I feel my fingers going away."

They weren't. Ava held his hand and counted his fingers with her thumb back and forth as his eyes fluttered closed. As his words began to slur, "I . . . goin . . ." She wouldn't even leave his side when Adam said, "Ava, go tell Bubby something's wrong with him."

AVA WASN'T ALLOWED TO hold his hand at the hospital later. She wasn't even allowed to go. Later that night Kovi's mother called Elaine and yelled at her in Russian. Elaine hung up the phone and said to Ava, "Fear sounds the same in any language."

Sometime after all this Ava saw a moving truck in the parking lot of the apartment building. The movers wore face masks to counter the stench of that garbage summer. She watched until she saw them bring out the hand-me-down dining set and then she rode away. Her handlebars were wrapped in squishy foam for comfort, and grasping them reminded her of holding Kovi's hand that night. How she had counted his fingers back and forth, making sure that he didn't leave.

Joy of Vicks

Inspired by *Purple America,*
Rick Moody

SHE WHO SITS AT her kitchen table across from her mother, who has flown in for the birth of this child; she who hears her mother's rattled, shaky cough, a chesty, phlegmy obstruction that sounds like guns popping as her mother's face turns red; she who gets up to fill a glass of water, to find the tissue box (which is empty because her household just finished a round of colds); she who passes her mother a torn paper towel instead; she who lets the water run cold so that it will refresh as it pushes back against the nagging cough, but really she who stands at the sink because she doesn't want to watch her mother spitting up the phlegm into the napkin, horking and gagging to battle against this cough that has probably been lingering for months. She who doesn't look, does not have to see.

She, who just started maternity leave, finally returns to the table and wonders when the wrinkles beneath her mother's eyes became as deep as bird footprints in snow, for how long has her mother's hand shaken like that? Exactly when did she turn into an old woman? She who takes a deep breath and feels the air moving unobstructed in and out of her lungs, silent and smooth. She who has managed this pregnancy without nausea, whose hair has grown thicker and shinier as the child develops within; she who looks at her mother's hair and sees where it is thinning, where her mother has teased and sprayed to give it body, to puff herself out, to mask what she is losing.

She who asks dumbly, "Have you seen your doctor?" and then wonders how many doctor's appointments there will be back home in the winter, her mother coughing at her own kitchen sink, and spitting out gobs of green gunk, spitting it down the drain, willing it to slide away, willing her head to stop spinning from breathing too fast and too shallow, standing there in an empty house, counting the steps to her car parked in a garage that is detached even though in the winter temperatures reach −40°C. She who thinks of her mother driving herself to her appointments, listening to the doctor's instructions for puffers and narcotic cough syrup and lung X-rays, and nights of her mother not sleeping as she sits up in her bed in her dark, still house, coughing against the echoes of colds and flus and dry coughs she once nursed for years before, the pulse of a house that at one time burst with the rhythm of a family healthy, then sick, then mending; children calling out to said mother in the middle of the night, "Mummy? Come lie with me."

She who remembers steamers and hot showers running for fifteen minutes in a closed bathroom, and Vicks VapoRub and medicine that tastes like sour cherries or spiked lemonade. She whose own house pulsates like that now, whose baby will be number three; whose mother, settled now from her coughing spasm, sips the lemon water with honey and says, "I'm fine. It's not that big a deal."

She who knows her mother is lying. She who is suddenly tired of being lied to. She who says back, "Why haven't you seen anyone? You can't breathe, for God's sake!"

Whose mother replies, "There's no one left to take me!"

She who sighs because they have always fought like this, blowing out a hot sigh, wordless notes on scales of frustration. She who can think of nothing else to say except "That's not an excuse"; who wants to pound the table and yell, *You don't get to choose not to look after yourself!* She who does not want to upset her mother in the first hour of this visit, who instead sits back in her chair, rubs her swollen belly while her mother starts coughing again, while she spits out honey lemon water that lands in droplets like blinking eyes on the table between them.

She who thought they would walk the Promenade Mall this afternoon to try to induce labour, who had pictured her mother flying in to rub her back against the Braxton Hicks contractions; she who has two best friends who have both buried mothers, who drove mothers to appointments, who took notes, who made soups and spoon-fed their mothers in hospital beds set up in childhood bedrooms; who were exhausted at the end of each day from waiting and resisting and knowing and wishing and praying and hoping and fighting and carrying and caring and soothing and witnessing and rubbing and crying and counting and waiting.

She who for the first time wonders which visit will be her mother's last.

SHE WHO WALKS HER mother up the stairs to her daughter's bedroom, to a bed overflowing with stuffed animals, whose daughter will sleep with her in her room on the floor in a sleeping bag; she who takes an armful of stuffies off the bed and piles them on the floor so that they look like a cartoon shot of zoo creatures piling up to escape an enclosure; she who pulls back the covers to her daughter's bed, as she does every night, but she who tucks her mother inside it, whose mother's eyes are closed before they hit the pillow; she who leans over to kiss the side of her mother's face, the wrinkles like a map of pathways that have brought her here to this bed, the lilac duvet cover, the unicorn poster taped on the wall above, the blind she is lowering so that the sun does not disturb her mother, whose shoulders shake from the cough that clings to her insides; she who leaves the room and closes the door and tries to remember where she put the humidifier and if she's changed the filter lately and whether she should fill the basin with water from the tub and then plug it in to steam her daughter's lilac and blue room that they just painted last summer because her daughter is eight now and has opinions.

She who wonders about calling her sister in Phoenix, her brother in Chicago, who thinks it's time to say, *What do we do about Mum?* She who imagines her brother on his bad cellphone connection saying, *It's just a cold*. Her sister saying, *She should use oil of oregano*, but pronouncing it *o-re-GAN-o* because she works in a health food store. She who feels her baby shift and push against her insides, which are tightening around his growing limbs (she who knows this baby is a boy but has told no one, but now wonders if she should tell her mother, just so they can share something). She who feels like pushing and pulling her way out of this house, even as she crouches by the bathtub, moves the plastic toys away from the faucet, fills the steamer so that she is doing something, hears more coughing from her daughter's bedroom and with each gasp wants to bolt. She who carries in the steamer, the Vicks, more pillows to prop up her mother's pale head; she who says, "Mum, let's give this a try."

She who dips her fingers into the eucalyptus Vaseline, who coughs herself from the sharp scent, who spreads the jelly on her mother's chest across her collarbone, who pulls down the V-neck T-shirt so as not to get it dirty. She who wants not to look but sees anyway, her mother's breasts, shrivelled and empty from nursing a long time ago, deflated against her pretty bra; she who feels both sadness and relief that her mother would still choose such a bra — an eggshell blue, a vine of flowers from the padded cups to the shoulder straps. She who keeps rubbing, stays away from her mother's breasts and instead kneads the leathery skin stretched across her chest, the top of her rib cage. She who feels the jagged breath rattling in and out of her mother's rib cage and presses deeper into her flesh as if the pressure might suppress it. She who begins to feel the humidity in the room rising, who watches the droplets form on the base of the window beneath the blind, who feels her mother relax beneath her touch, whose mother takes her first deep breath, who lets one tear roll down her cheek at the joy of having made a difference.

Like Landing
the Gimli Glider

ISAAC IS NOT SURE how he ended up in his car, being directed by his nine-year-old grandniece.

"Park around the corner," Ava tells him. She wraps a red leash around her hand like a bandage, winding it tight until the tips of her fingers turn red.

"You're not supposed to take something that isn't yours," Isaac says, pulling over the curb. How could she have missed this lesson? Doesn't Elaine send her to that Jewish day school? Isaac never went to Jewish day school, but he knew the Ten Commandments. Especially number eight: Thou shalt not steal.

"His owners aren't looking after him," Ava said, looking out the side window at the sidewalk. "This isn't stealing, it's rescuing."

The entitlement. But still he sits there with her, puts the car in park.

"There he is!" Ava calls out, opening the car door before Isaac can grab her arm. Is that what he's supposed to do, as her great-uncle and not her parent? She's running up the sidewalk, yelling, "Cookie! Come here, Cookie!" and she's waving the leash like it's something a dog should come running toward, not away from.

But Cookie does indeed approach Ava. He is one of those tiny dogs that remind Isaac of the petite, skinny mothers he sees at the Promenade Mall when it's too cold for him to walk the neighbourhood. The ones with double strollers and cup holders for their Aroma lattes. They have high voices and throw their heads back when they're laughing. Cookie and Ava chase each other around one of the trees near the curb. Cookie crouches with his bum up in the air, his tail wagging. Ava laughs, crouching down in front of his pointy face, curling her finger at him and whispering. He leaps into her arms to lick her nose and chin and cheeks.

She drapes the leash over her arm and walks back to the car, cradling this dog like a baby. Isaac looks up and down the street. No one has come after the dog. Ava says, "See? They're not looking after him. He's been loose for days."

She had first told him this when he was crouched beside her amongst all her Legos on Elaine's living room floor. She was playing with a set designed to be a veterinarian's office. The little Lego people were all girls, with the same plastic hairstyle in different colours—blond, red, black, poofy around the head and then curled up at the bottom just past their shoulders.

One of them had her arm stretched out to pat a pony and there was a white rabbit lying at her feet.

Ava said they had to save this dog because otherwise he could get hit by a car. Or kidnapped. When Isaac said, "I guess when you put it that way," she threw her arms around him and squealed, "Oh my God! You're the best!"

. . .

HAD ISAAC GIVEN IN too early to his younger sister? There was nothing drawing him back to Toronto and it's not as if he'd left on good terms, fifty years ago. A lifetime of births and deaths, of people from his family growing up and leaving and only knowing him through photographs, postcards, the odd trip in for a wedding or bar mitzvah. Before Thornhill, this suburb north of Toronto, Isaac lived in Melbourne, Israel, New York, Barcelona, Singapore. For the last three years he lived in L.A., selling protein powder and bars for a friend through eBay, renting his friend's apartment with a terracotta patio and a palm tree for shade. He was sitting out on that patio, shirt untucked, forehead sweating from the intense morning sun, when he got the call from Elaine. She was sobbing. And Isaac's younger sister never sobbed. Not after her daughter, Carly, left the kids to take a trip to Las Vegas with some girlfriends and then decided not to come back.

Not after her husband of almost forty years died of an aneurysm soon after that. Elaine got quiet when she was sad. Resigned. She would say things like "I have to be strong for the kids."

But this sobbing Elaine sounded completely different. She was crying so hard she was hiccupping.

"I'm all they've got and that's not enough. They need more family."

"They have each other. Like we did."

"What if something happens to me, Isaac? What if I'm the next one to go?"

"Are you sick? Lainy, what are you telling me?" Be it God, karma, or the universe, Isaac had had enough of the injustices lobbed at his sister, a woman who did nothing but make sure the people she loved were looked after. When would she be rewarded?

She'd stopped crying and taken a deep breath. Isaac heard her exhale slowly. She took another breath and cleared her throat.

"I'm telling you that I need your help. For just a little while. You don't have to live with me. My seamstress has a basement apartment. But you could be here for meals. Maybe you could take the kids out every once in a while."

"You want me to move there?"

She went quiet. He imagined her in her kitchen, her table covered in the morning's newspaper, the kids' breakfast dishes still in front of their seats. Elaine with one hand holding the phone receiver to her ear, the other holding her forehead.

"Isaac, I've never asked you for anything."

When their father was sick and Isaac was in Australia, she never once said, *Why aren't you here?* Isaac still owed his father money, and if Elaine knew, she never asked where it was or when he planned to pay back the estate. She never once questioned when he would settle down, never implied — as others had — that his solitary life was somehow worth less than hers.

"I just can't imagine what I could do to help." But then again, he knew he owed it to her to try. Not that he ever felt he owed anything to anyone. Nor could he explain why he felt that way now.

· · ·

"NOW YOU NEED TO drive your car," Ava tells him.

"And just where am I supposed to go?"

"I don't know. You were supposed to figure that out. We can't go home yet. Bubby's not going to let me in with a dog. And even if I hide him in my room, Adam will tell on me."

"You haven't thought this through."

Cookie wiggles out of Ava's arms. He whines, stretching his neck toward Isaac. Isaac's throat begins to tighten. He wishes he were back in L.A. Or Melbourne. Or New York City. Or any of the many places he's lived or visited alone in his seventy-two years.

On top of Cookie's whining, Ava has started to cry. Her face is buried in the dog's back. Now Isaac can see what he hadn't noticed before: They look alike, their scraggily unbrushed hair/fur, oily and knotted, hanging in clumps. Their thick bellies, their begging eyes. Ava says, "Uncle Isaac, please. We need to look after him. You need to help me."

Driving, Isaac thinks of Elaine. When she's dealing with Ava and Adam, she looks so much like their mother did—her wrinkled forehead, the lines by her eyes and mouth turned down when the kids tattle on each other. He thinks about his niece, Carly, who was raised in this supposedly good neighbourhood. But even people from good neighbourhoods make shitty choices. He thinks about how Ava probably cries at night in Elaine's house, in Carly's old bedroom, how there are nights he finds himself crying too, up late watching something on the History Channel. Like the documentary about the Gimli Glider, the story of a plane in 1983 going from Montreal to Edmonton that ran out of fuel and the pilot glided it safely onto the runway of the tiny airport in Gimli, Manitoba. There he is, bawling like a baby at the pilot's bravery, his heroism. How he could step up at just the right moment. By the time he's reached his apartment with Ava and Cookie, he's wondering why she shouldn't have some happiness. And maybe that's why he's here.

. . .

ISAAC'S RUSSIAN LANDLADY, Mona, is away for the
weekend, so when Cookie barks and runs around the
basement, Isaac turns to Ava and says, "I'll take you
home and he can stay with me for one night. But by
tomorrow you have to have permission to keep him."

"I will," she says. "Bubby said we could get a dog
sometime. And I'm gonna train him. She won't even
know he's there."

Before Isaac takes her back home, Ava sits on the
floor and rubs Cookie's tummy. She tells Isaac about
her gymnastics class on Sundays, about how she's in the
most advanced level with all the older girls. Back in
L.A., Isaac had some friends with grandchildren. They
talked about their levels—in school (the reading!), in
music (Mozart! At her age!), in swimming (in the deep
end! She's only five!). One had a granddaughter who
was Olympic material. Isaac thinks, *Hey, look! Me too!
Did you ever think?*

"Can I show you my splits?" Ava asks, and then she
stretches her legs out, but she's no gymnast. Her back
leg is bent; she's high off the ground. Isaac can see that
she's as far down as she can get and she's holding her
breath so that her face turns red from trying.

"Hey," he says. "Yeah, that's really good." She just
needs to practise. Everyone starts out somewhere. Isaac
once saw a cover of a notebook that said, *Don't compare*

your beginning to someone else's middle. He should show Ava that. In case she's been comparing.

Ava sits back down on the floor and Cookie puts his head in her lap. She smiles up at Isaac and says, "You'll come to my show at the end of the year. The parents come to watch us do our gymnastics. Grandparents too. But I'll be the only one there with an uncle!"

"Sure!" Isaac says. Maybe he'll even take a picture on his cellphone. Send it to the friend of the future Olympian.

THE NEXT MORNING, Elaine pounds on his door at 9 a.m. Since coming to Toronto, Isaac has not woken up before eleven. Cookie snores in the bed beside him. He sounds like he's growling, like he could wake up ready to attack. Elaine is screaming.

"Isaac! Open up right now! I know you can hear me!"

He has never heard her under the influence of such fury. He sits up in bed before opening his eyes. His heart beats in his chest in sync with Elaine's fist at his door. But the actual sound of it all is muffled, as if she's screaming at him through a pillow.

On the other side of the door, Isaac finds not only Elaine but a sobbing Ava, her arms crossed, her nose blotchy red and running.

"For heaven's sake," he says. "You want to wake the neighbours?"

Elaine looks down at Cookie, wagging his tail, jumping up on his hind legs. "Oh my God."

Ava, despite her tears, falls onto her knees and smiles as Cookie licks her wet, salty face.

"See?" she says. "I told you he loves me."

"I can't believe you went along with this," Elaine says. She doesn't take off her coat, or move from the entranceway at the top of the basement stairs. Isaac's feet are cold from the linoleum floor, the late-November air coming through the side door, which was not closed properly. He shifts his weight from side to side, stepping up and down, like a runner warming up on the spot. She sounds so much like their mother yelling at him about the money he owed. His tongue feels just as heavy now as it did back then, the weight of all his excuses.

"Honestly." Elaine keeps talking. "What were you thinking? What were you going to tell the cops when they came to arrest you for stealing?"

"This isn't stealing," Isaac tells her. "It's rescuing."

"Oh my God!"

"The dog was outside all on his own. It's better than me taking him to the pound. It would have been irresponsible for us to just leave him there."

Elaine walks into the apartment, past Ava and Cookie and over to the small folding table and chairs Isaac has set up in his main room. She sits down and leans forward with her elbows on the table, her head in her hands. She rubs her forehead with her fingers. From behind, it looks as if she's nodding her head.

"Have you lost your mind?" She sighs, turning around, her head tilted to one side. She looks at him like she does at her grandchildren — tired, fed up, those sagging cheeks, her downturned, disappointed mouth.

Isaac did not ask to be tested like this. He never loses his mind. In his experience, people only say that when they refuse to see your point of view. Elaine had to know all along that Isaac was never coming here to conform. She asked for his help, which he can only give in his way.

"This isn't about me," he tells her. Didn't Ava tell him the dog was in danger? Practically homeless? "This is about doing what's right. It's about saving this dog from getting hit by a car!"

"Uncle Isaac." Ava says his name and then hiccups. "Bubby said if I take Cookie back and apologize, we can talk about getting a dog of our own."

Elaine stretches out her arm toward Ava with the red leash dangling. "Ava, take Cookie outside to pee before he messes all over your uncle's floor. You can wait for me out there."

After Ava leaves, Isaac says, "So why are you letting her get a dog, then? Where's the lesson in that?"

Elaine doesn't look at him when she stands up. Isaac feels the silence in his apartment like a blanket settling over his head. Elaine finally says, "She's the nine-year-old. You're the adult. I didn't bring you here to complicate my life."

"I didn't ask you to bring me here!"

In his mind, he is already reaching for his suitcase to leave before Elaine can tell him to go. That's how he did it years ago, bag in hand, out the door into a taxi before his mother could hear the front door close.

. . .

THAT NIGHT, ISAAC WATCHES *Rear Window,* with James Stewart and Grace Kelly. He loves the shadows in the film, like a puppet show. He imagines Hitchcock pulling the strings of his actors as he dances them across the set, and only James Stewart sitting there the whole time, not moving. An entire movie played from a single chair. That whole notion of seeing something you can't explain—and having no one to explain it to.

He picks up the phone and calls Elaine, even though it is after ten o'clock. Tomorrow is the first night of Chanukah. He's supposed to be with her and the kids. When she answers, he says, "Maybe I shouldn't come tomorrow."

He pictures Elaine lying in the middle of her double bed, duvet pulled up to her chin, watching the news. Every night Elaine watches CBC, even though Isaac's told her they're anti-Israel and that she's better off watching CNN. But she swears by that Peter Mansbridge anchor. Isaac can hear his authoritative baritone in the background when Elaine answers, "If you don't come, where does that leave me?"

"I don't know what you want from me."

"I shouldn't have to deal with all this on my own. And you shouldn't be alone either."

"I never said I was lonely."

Except that Isaac has always viewed loneliness as his most constant friend. He always thought the only surety in life was to count on yourself.

"Do you know what it's like listening to all my friends brag about the trouble they have fitting their expanding families in their dining rooms for holidays? If you don't come tomorrow, it's going to be me making latkes for the kids and that's it. I wouldn't even bother setting the dining room table."

"I don't even know what to bring for the kids."

"Just get them gift cards to Toys'R'Us. Or maybe one from PetSmart for Ava. We're getting a dog in the new year."

"You are?" Isaac can only picture Cookie, as if there is no other dog to be had.

"Yes. Cookie's owners live right across the street. They were worried sick about him. At least Ava sees that now. I'll get her a stupid dog. When she and Adam are smiling, I feel like maybe I'm not screwing up their lives."

Isaac knows he is not making this any better. He only makes things harder for her. He'll go over tomorrow, one last time, his suitcase in the car, and they'll never realize when he drives off at the end what he really meant when he said goodbye.

"None of this is your fault, Lainy."

Elaine doesn't answer right away. In the background Isaac hears sirens from her TV. They sound tinny — like they're ringing from inside a can. She whispers, "Thank you for saying that." She sighs. "You see? This is why I need you here."

It's like she's taken the suitcase out of his hand. She's steered him back inside. She's closed the door behind him and he didn't even hear the bolt lock click into place.

· · ·

MANY YEARS AGO, before he left Toronto, Isaac dated a girl he quite liked. She was bookish. She knew her literature. They watched good films together. There weren't too many girls he considered his intellectual equal, but she was. And pretty. She had a soft face that rested in a smile when she was listening.

Once, she invited him over to meet her parents. He remembers that after supper, she went to lie down on the couch in the living room. He brought his plate into the kitchen. Her mother was impressed with his manners. Had he proposed, her parents would have pushed her to say yes. He came out of the kitchen and saw her father kneeling on the floor beside the couch, hand on his daughter's cheek, as if she were a child about to fall asleep. When Isaac remembers this now, it's not that he remembers being disturbed. The intimacy wasn't obscene. But the raw display of affection from both of them, well, it was odd. He knew then that he would never feel that way toward her. More so, he could never be that kind of father, and she would expect that of the man she married.

The next day he broke it off between them. They went for coffee. He did it nicely—not like they do today with texting. He meant her no harm nor disrespect. He doesn't remember her crying. She asked him why and he told her straight out, "I can't be something that I'm not."

And that's the thing with Elaine and Ava. They both want him to be this hero. He really thought he could—at least for Ava. Saving that stupid dog. And he liked the way she looked at him, like helping her was as good as saving the world. That was the look the girlfriend had shared with her father. Isaac never thought he wanted to be that person, but now here he was. And for heaven's sake, hasn't Ava had enough disappointments?

It's the middle of the night, hours since he spoke with his sister. Isaac lies awake and for the umpteenth time thinks how he should never have agreed to come. Now he has to live up to that look, and he never asked for that.

. . .

ISAAC DRIVES TO ELAINE's for the Chanukah dinner with the two cards for Ava and Adam on the passenger seat beside him. They are both light blue and Isaac is wondering why Chanukah colours have to be blue and white, the colours of the Israeli flag. Isaac lived in Israel when he was in his mid-twenties. He worked in the fields on a kibbutz. He ate red tomatoes and green cucumbers for breakfast with white sour yogurt. At Chanukah no one exchanged gifts. They just ate sufganiot, jelly doughnuts covered in white powdered sugar. Back then, it made him think of Canada and the snow-covered sidewalks, his sister Elaine and her girlfriends giggling as they slid along the ice in their wool coats, clutching each other's arms. But he didn't miss it. Instead, he felt the soft dough of the fresh pastry on his tongue, the sugar melting as soon as it touched his lips, the warmth of a room full of people with hands stained brown from the sun and the mud, like those Maccabee warriors from the Chanukah story, living in the hills, planning something wonderful.

When Isaac hits the dog, turning onto Elaine's street, he thinks he's hit a squirrel.

"Shit," he says as he drives up the road, parks beside the curve outside Elaine's house. Those damn creatures dart out into the streets always at the wrong time, like they're playing chicken. He didn't even have a chance to react. A flash and then a thud and then the slight bump under his tires. In L.A., Isaac once saw a coyote lying by the side of the highway, its fur blown up by the desert wind, its mouth open slightly, as if in mid-snarl. But the rest of its body was flat, as if the stuffing had been removed. As Isaac drove on then, he thought, *Well, at least it wasn't someone's pet.*

And now, Isaac jumps out of his car and runs back down the icy street, calling, "Cookie!" before he can stop anything from coming out of his mouth. Even at this distance, he can tell that the dog is on his side, his body flattened. Isaac bends down where Cookie lies curled on the road, blood pooling from his mouth and around his tongue, flopped to the side. The blood is dark, almost black against the pavement.

"Stupid dog," Isaac says, kneeling down on the ground, putting his hand on Cookie's back. He can feel the dog's cracked ribs, and then he notices the way the legs are splayed, twisted like Ava's splits.

"Shit," he says again. "Shit, shit, shit."

From down the block, Isaac hears someone call his name. He looks up and can just make out Ava's silhouette on Elaine's driveway. She's frozen on the spot. She's just in a T-shirt and leggings. Her voice sounds small and light when she calls out, "Is that you?"

Isaac gets up and calls back, "Go back inside. I just thought I hit a squirrel."

"Did you?"

He stands directly in front of Cookie. "No, it's alright. I didn't. Go on back in."

He watches her walk back up the driveway, sees the screen door open and then close as she steps inside. He turns back to the dog and takes off his scarf to wrap around the body. He has no idea where to take him, or whose door to knock on. He'll have to tell Elaine quietly, in the kitchen, away from Ava, who will be playing Lego, using that plastic vet hospital, saving those plastic animal lives. He picks up the dog and moves him onto the grass, burying him beneath a pile of leaves. Cookie's face is distorted from the impact. His snout is twisted. Isaac's leather driving gloves get wet and clammy from arranging the pile — dead foliage, dead dog, and now with the wet leather he smells like wet animal. He tells himself that Ava will have forgotten about Cookie with the new dog coming. Kids know how to move on. And he promised her he'd attend that gymnastics recital. She'll tell everyone there that he's her uncle. Before he turns away to go into the house, Isaac mutters at the pile, "You should have stayed home."

Loose Change

BARB IS CROUCHED in her bedroom closet when she hears the front door open. Janelle calls up, "Mum?" and Barb immediately wonders what Janelle will be wearing. If it's dress pants, then she's only popping in on her way to the clinic. If it's jeans, then Barb has her for the day. She can't decide which would be better. She can tell by the sharpness of the edge in Janelle's voice that her daughter is already annoyed, like she's come prepared for Barb to do something stupid. That's their routine—Janelle finding ways to remind Barb that she (the daughter) is the smarter one.

Barb has been counting pennies. She is at 664. When she gets to 700, she will call back down.

"Mum?"

Now Janelle's voice is more urgent. Perhaps even concerned? But Barb is afraid of losing her place. There must be at least five boxes filled with pennies in her closet. She already found two quarters and six nickels in the first box. Janelle is running up the stairs now because Barb hasn't answered. She knows it's not fair to make Janelle worried, but this is the push/pull of their lifelong power struggle. And Barb has to exert some control at the beginning of their visits because she always loses her grasp by the end. She sits back and counts Janelle's steps, the pounding up the stairs. The barometric rise in her daughter's panic. Janelle's panic reminds Barb of a sudden summer storm coming out of nowhere, like the time Kevin screamed for Barb from the basement. Mild-mannered Kevin who tried to wake the dead.

"For God's sake, Mum! What are you doing?"

Barb looks up. She's hunched over. Her shoulders hurt from not moving. She twists her neck slowly to turn her face toward her daughter. Janelle is pale, the lines between her eyebrows pronounced. She's wearing her black dress pants that Barb told her ages ago were too big.

"I didn't want to lose count," Barb tells her.

"You were supposed to have his clothes ready for me."

"I haven't done his suits, or the drawers. I need to do the drawers."

Janelle exhales. "And you haven't because . . . ?"

"Don't be smart with me," Barb says, but she knows from the floor she doesn't look nearly as stern as she wants to, especially cross-legged, surrounded by pennies.

"Do you have to do this now?" Janelle asks. It's the same tone Barb has heard her use with her boys when they start Lego projects just before bed. Barb tries not to smirk the way she's seen them do when they know they've outsmarted their mother.

She moves onto her knees, knocking over her latest tower of ten coins. She says, "Shit," and Janelle says, "Honestly."

Barb's knees burn as she rises. She looks down so that she doesn't disturb any more of the pennies as she tiptoes out of the closet. They even remind her of the boys' Lego cities, mini towers like high rises, like the outline of the Toronto skyline, but this time glimmering copper. She wants to say to Janelle, *But look what I made!*

Janelle says, "I told you to have everything ready for me in bags by your bedroom door."

"So come back later."

"I am. With Natasha. She's good at what she does, but she can't stage the house unless you get it ready first."

"I'm not the one in the rush," Barb says. Seven hundred pennies and that's just a dent in the first box. She hasn't even looked in the others. What if Charlie arranged them by value? What if the last one is full of loonies and toonies?

Janelle grabs the bag of shoes. She's pouting. She always juts her chin out when she's losing an argument.

Her chin and her flared nostrils. Charlie used to joke she was like an animal in the wild, always on guard.

Janelle says, "Just hide the bags from Natasha. Maybe in the closet. I'll take them when we're done."

"It's not that I can't let this stuff go," Barb says, but Janelle is already heading down the stairs, the bag of shoes bumping down each step, like not just one but a hundred people running out the door.

. . .

TWO SUMMERS AGO, Barb and Charlie took *The Canadian* out west. It was supposed to be their first of many retirement trips. She found him one night, sitting in the lounge car for the sleeper-class passengers at the back of the train. Plush booth seating was on either side of the car, facing the centre so that groups of people could congregate. But Charlie was by himself. There were windows all around, but they were riding through the Saskatchewan prairie, so everything was deep black. Except for the moon, which hung high in the sky like a lone but dim light bulb. Charlie stretched his arm over the back of the seat. He stared past his hand, out the back window, like he had forgotten something. She very rarely saw her husband lost in thought. Charlie was always moving forward, purposeful. She caught her breath at the sight of his vulnerability. She was sur-prised, even then, at how much she loved him.

Barb wore only her nightgown. The air condition-
ing blew up her legs. She stood with her knees pressed
together because she didn't have underwear on. Even
though no one could tell, she still felt indecent, all that
cold air blowing up to her crotch.

She said, "You need to come to bed."

Charlie looked over at her, startled — as if he was
not only surprised to see her just then, but on the train
at all. She wondered if perhaps he had been sleeping,
upright, his body rocking with the jerky train. He
blinked and then said, "I've never felt more awake."

Barb sat down beside him, placed her head on his
collarbone. The train lurched and rocked. He held her
side but turned his head back to stare out the window.
There was something timeless about travelling in the
dark. Like there was no tomorrow and they were being
propelled backwards. Ageless.

· · ·

AFTER JANELLE LEAVES, Barb doesn't pack Charlie's
sweaters. She flings them around the room. She tosses
them up in the air and lets them fall like dead birds,
one at a time. She read once about birds falling from
the sky, somewhere in B.C., their bodies weighed down
and coated in slick oil. Or was that the news report
about the gulls and fish washing up on the Pacific shore
after a tanker spill? Barb could never keep these earthly

tragedies straight. Charlie would have remembered. Charlie would have picked up each sweater she was throwing and quietly explained the correct story to her, like talking down a child mid-tantrum. But in his absence, Barb kicks at his fallen clothes, allows herself to be that angry child, the one who would step on those dead birds just to feel the crunch beneath her feet.

Then, as if she has suddenly heard a noise — like a caw, something snapping, or the sound of a handful of coins tumbling to the floor — Barb turns again toward her closet. She's willing to bet that whole first box of pennies that Charlie stacked the collection in order of value. She goes back inside the closet and moves the boxes one by one until she gets to the last one. Then she lifts the lid and lets out a laugh so full of weight, glory, and self-righteousness that she scares herself. But there she is, that greedy, heartless child, digging her hands into her treasure trove of loonies and toonies; that catch in the depths of her stomach telling her if she isn't fast, someone (calmer, more forward-thinking, practical) will come and take this prize away.

• • •

WEEKS AGO, NATASHA SHOWED Barb a condo she could rent for two years. Barb wouldn't have to commit to buying until she knew she wanted that lifestyle. Janelle was there too. The condo was in midtown

Toronto, near Lawrence and Bathurst, twenty minutes south from the suburban two-storey detached
home Barb had lived in for the past thirty-five years,
the last year on her own. Immediately Barb thought
the building was too religious for her. There was a
plaque beside the elevator indicating which one would
be on Sabbath mode for Friday nights and Saturdays.
While they were waiting to go up to see the condo,
a young couple came out of the elevator with a large
double stroller. He wore a black velvet *kippah*, she a
very shiny brown wig that could have passed for a
real head of hair.

Janelle said, "I know lots of people in this building,
Mum. They're not all like that."

Barb asked, "At Passover, does the wallpaper in the
hallways peel off from the stench of gefilte fish?"

Janelle muttered, "Give me a break." But Natasha
didn't know better. She said, "I doubt that. They keep
this building in excellent condition."

They got into the elevator and Janelle finally added,
"For God's sake, Mum. This isn't 1950s Montreal. No
one makes gefilte fish from scratch anymore."

When they got into the unit, Janelle went straight
to the living room window and said, "See, Mum? You
can see my place right over there. The boys can wave
to you when they're playing outside."

Barb looked out that window and knew she'd be
getting phone calls. *Can you see the boys? Can you just*

watch them? Janelle said, "Did I tell you about my colleague, the other doctor in the practice? She's Filipino. Can you believe her parents look after her three kids full time? She says it's just part of their culture."

Barb heard the incredulity in her voice but also the question. Janelle was always setting her up like this. They only ended up disappointing each other.

"Yes," Barb said. "Well. That must be why they're so good at looking after people. Isn't your nanny from the Philippines?"

Janelle answered quickly, her voice rising. "She is. I was just saying. It's interesting, different cultures."

Natasha walked through the unit, her heels ticking loudly against the parquet floor. A plane flew over. Barb watched it descend in the distance. There was no balcony with this unit, but Barb daydreamed about leaping off one anyway. Not to fall or plummet, but to fly, following the plane on its tailwinds.

"Is that the airport over there?" she asked.

"Oh, it's quite a ways away. You won't be bothered by any noise," Natasha promised.

"I don't mind," Barb said, turning away from the window. "I always liked to fly."

· · ·

BARB DRIVES WITH THE boxes resting side by side on her back seat. She uses the seat belts to hold them in place.

Even still, the coins jostle when she goes over speed bumps, when she makes a right turn onto Bathurst, and then again as she follows the curve of the on-ramp for the 407. She had expected a note from Charlie in one of the boxes, a hint, something to indicate what his intentions were for the money. She remembers at the end of the day how he would empty his pants pockets into a dish on their dresser, the coins chiming against the stoneware. Sometimes he kept a pack of gum in there too. Even now, the dish smells like mint. She gets a whiff of it in the morning, when she opens her underwear drawer. She never thought about what happened to the coins when the dish was full. After all, it was just loose change.

She checks the clock on her dashboard and she giggles. This is just like Charlie. Seizing opportunity. Like after the summer train trip, how he decided he wanted a pair of real train seats to finish off his basement lounge. The walls above them were covered in old VIA, CN, and CP plaques he'd collected that read *Spitting prohibited*, *No standing in the vestibule*. There was a poster of the silver *Canadian* cutting through the Rockies. The mountains had been spectacular, but when Barb thinks back on their trip, what she remembers most is the contrast between the open, clear sky of the prairies and those fields after fields of yellow canola. She remembers feeling like they were riding through a blank canvas. There was just so much possibility.

Charlie found Kevin online on some train forum. Kevin worked at a train yard not far from their house. He said he could source train seats from a retired car. When he showed up at the house with the seats in the back of his truck, Charlie danced a jig on the driveway. Barb stood on the front steps with her arms folded, trying hard to look disapproving, but she had to bite her bottom lip to keep from laughing. And sweet Kevin smiled bashfully at the ground. He reminded Barb of one of her students from when she taught high-school French — a basketball player named Dan, quiet, tall, large hands. Helpful. Once, the boy helped her move her desk across the classroom.

Charlie and Kevin were such a study in contrasts as they carried those heavy steel seat frames out of the truck and down to the basement. Kevin's young muscles bulged with confidence. Charlie's old arms quivered. Of course, once they set the seats on the floor, Charlie had to sit down to have a rest. He had no business lifting those seats in the first place. It's no wonder his heart stopped beating beneath the poster that proclaimed *Breathtaking scenery.*

• • •

BARB WALKS INTO THE airport with the boxes of coins stacked on one of those luggage carts, along with her blue overnight bag. Her own heart flutters. She should have gone to the bank first and she laughs at herself because what is she thinking? The coins jingle as she pushes her cart. She passes families travelling with carts piled with suitcases. The scene reminds her of the holidays, the faint sound of bells, all those expectations.

There are no customers at the ticket counter and Barb realizes she's never bought a ticket this way before. Impulsively. They always booked their travel through an agent, with Charlie making the call. For the train trip, they sat in the travel agency office, pamphlets on the table between them and the agent, a woman who was Barb's age. The agent arranged their train tickets right then and said, "This is just the start for you. Your adventures together."

It was later that evening, with the pamphlets spread out on the kitchen table, that Barb took a call from a parent. She could hear his son, Dan the basketball player, crying in the background. Earlier that day, after he helped her move her desk, she found him smoking up in the back hall. Even now, she remembers his pale face, his blind panic, that wide-eyed look of wondering: *What is she going to do to me?*

"How dare you threaten my son?" the father said. Barb felt his venom like a crashing wave, the roar of water overhead. "There are scouts looking at him. You're just his French teacher."

"No one is allowed to break school rules. There are consequences."

"You can't fucking play with people's lives!" He raised his voice on "fucking." Barb felt her throat tighten, as if the father had reached through the phone and grabbed her neck.

"I will drag your name through the mud," the man said. "You report him and I will make sure you don't work anywhere, ever again."

Charlie was motioning for the phone while Barb was trying to wave him away. She couldn't even put a face to this irate man, so she pictured the boy, his forehead scattered with pimples, his back as well. He wore a sleeveless jersey and she remembered noticing the acne on his shoulders as he ran away from her. She was saying, "Now listen . . ." But then Charlie grabbed the phone and went on about how dare he. Barb was trying not to cry because she didn't want to be like that boy, dissolving in the background while someone else did the fixing. But she felt her chin jutting out while she pouted, while she breathed heavily through her nose, her flared nostrils.

When Charlie hung up the phone, he pointed at her and said, "Tomorrow you hand in your resignation and we take this trip together as retirees. I'm tired of assholes like him telling my wife how to do her job."

And Barb said, "Okay," because it was easier than arguing. It was always easier. But oh, did her insides burn. She busied herself with the pamphlets, but she felt such hate, and not toward the father, or Charlie, or even that weak, useless boy. She hated how easily she always gave up. And so she burned with hatred for herself. Her fingers shook as she flipped through pages of grey-haired couples, their reflections in the train windows, the sun softening their smiling, worry-free faces.

. . .

NOW BARB STANDS in front of the ticket counter. The agent has long nails, bright pink, and they click at her keyboard, like Natasha's heels, like the echo in the condo Barb has just realized she won't be taking. Barb is thinking of the airplane taking off, of it flying over Janelle's house, the boys running around in the backyard, the nanny on her cellphone not looking up when the plane roars overhead. The boys jumping and waving and Barb waving back through one of those thick, tiny windows, waving over the boys, the roof of that empty condo, Janelle racing along the highway to the airport when she realizes what her mother has done. Barb blowing kisses.

The woman looks up and smiles. "Can I help you?" Barb says, "Yes. I'm ready to go."

The Greatest Love Story
Never Told

Draft One

Sol was looking after his granddaughter, Jessica, a fourteen-year-old dancer who had broken her ankle in her last competition. She and her mother had recently moved into his house because of the divorce. There were still boxes piled like collapsed pyramids all over the place. Jessie lay on the coach eating potato chips and watching one of those trashy soap operas, the kind of show his Bella used to watch. His daughter, Hillary, hated that. The crappy TV, the crappy food. Before she left for work, she said to Sol, "Don't let Jessie lay around all day surrounded by junk."

It seemed to Sol that since the separation, his daughter had taken to barking orders, the way a dog lashes out when it feels threatened.

Sol turned to Jessica and said, "So, do you want to hear the real story of how I met your grandmother?"

She shifted on the couch so that she was sitting up. She brushed the crumbs from her lap and licked her fingers, nodding her head. The couple on the screen were kissing surrounded by lit candles, a bed made with satin sheets, the woman's blond head tilted back, the man's hand lost in her hair. Sol turned off the TV and said, "I'd be a skeleton in a cave right now if it wasn't for her."

Edits

Hillary used to have two last names, but a couple of weeks ago she decided to drop her soon-to-be ex's. When she told Sol, he said, "So does that mean I can just cut your business card in half?"

She cried in response. She blew her nose and then whispered, "You know that's what Mum would have said."

But tonight when she called from the office, she was yelling. It sounded to Sol like she'd been yelling even before he answered the phone. "What the hell did you tell her?"

"Who?"

"Jessica. What did you tell her, Dad? About Mum. Mum was your saviour? That never happened."

"Says who?" Sol's heart was beating so loudly it muffled the truth inside his head.

"You lied to her!"

"I wouldn't ever lie about your mother!"

"Are you losing your mind? Do I have to call Dr. Herman?"

"It's my story, Hillary," Sol said. He had never, until now, thought about taking ownership of his story. *History*.

"Don't start with me."

"One day, when Jessica asks about you and Daniel, you'll tell your story. And you'll remember things you could never have told her before —"

"This has nothing to do with me and Daniel!"

" — And you'll watch her listening to you, so you'll keep talking. I wasn't lying. Stories always change," Sol said.

"We all miss her, Dad. But it doesn't help imagining her in places she never was."

Sol set the portable on the counter and looked around the kitchen. He knew the difference between here and gone. He could tell an empty room when he was in it. Who was she — who was anyone — to tell him what didn't help?

Draft Two

There are train tracks that run behind Jessie's new house, the payoff for the long backyard, which she's now too old to even appreciate. She lies awake because of the discomfort in her ankle, a pain that feels like stretching even when she's trying to relax. And the way it stretches—one fibre pulling on another and then another; how that crawls up her leg like the train rumbling past the back of her house, waking her up in the middle of the night. Is it the train or the ankle? That sound of the wheels ka-klunking over rail joints and Jessie imagining with each klunk the pain in her ankle climbing a ladder, rung by rung, up her leg.

She hates this house. She can never get comfortable here. Even the couch in front of the TV is off; it's the same one that was in her basement in the other house on Spring Gate, but in this house it feels stiff. Like it's holding in its guts because it barely fits in the room, because all these rooms are smaller than what they had before.

When they agreed to move in, Hillary said, "Hey, there's a park two blocks away!"

They were with Zaida Sol for supper, eating Chinese takeout from Cynthia's, the restaurant on Bathurst Street with the pink sign and fairy lights all year round. Sol said, "You used to love the swings!"

"Now they make me nauseous," Jessie told them. Her mother should have known that. Or at least realized that everything about this change in the family has left Jessie feeling dizzy and imbalanced all the time.

· · ·

After the dance competition, Jessica was on crutches for the rest of the school year. She had flubbed her tap solo on stage and fell hard, her arms flailing, the stage lights capturing the magenta sequence stripe on her tin soldier costume. Her hat fell forward while she fell back, landing on her ankle twisted beneath her bum. All the other girls in her group drew in their breath in unison, but Jessica remembered Sarah's face. It looked like she was smiling beneath her hands covering her mouth.

Sol had been in the audience. Jessica knew that he often described her to his friends as like a deer—not caught in the headlights, but with the graceful movement of one who does not realize she is being watched. Her mother rushed to the stage when she fell, as the other girls began to circle around her while she cried out and clutched her foot. From the audience she heard her grandfather clapping, as if it was all part of the act. He even yelled out, "Encore!"

Jessica's dance group went on to win three dance competitions without her. Her friends posted photos, hovering around the trophies, their lips all the same shade of candy apple red. Two of the girls (Sarah was one of them) were allowed to wear fake eyelashes. Their eyes were wider than everyone else's. Popping.

Jessica presented her grandfather's story in her Social Studies class when they were talking about family geneology. She raised her hand and said, "My grandparents' story is a miracle." She started from the beginning, not remembering the names of the towns they came from, or that there were other boys with her grandfather in the woods. But before she got to the part where Sol and her grandmother meet again, her teacher told her to stand up in front of the class. She favoured her left side because of the walking cast, shifting her weight to that foot, her damaged leg bent at the knee, toe touching the floor behind her other heel. When she spoke, she didn't look at the other students directly, but focused on the back wall, the map of medieval England, a faded poster from the version of *Romeo and Juliet* with Leonardo DiCaprio.

There were gasps from her girlfriends when she came to the part about her grandfather recognizing her grandmother on that first date. Ava, who always had greasy hair and whose pants showed her butt crack, started to tear up. Jessica embellished the story. She said that they got engaged that night on a park bench, her grandfather proposing with a twist-tie he found on the ground that he wound to fit her grandmother's finger perfectly, the ends bent together into the shape of a heart. Ava raised her hand at the end and, with tears running down her face, asked if Jessica's grandmother had kept the original engagement ring.

"Yes," Jessica told her. When Ava cried, her face turned blotchy and accented her acne. "She would let me play with it in her bedroom. I was never allowed to unwind it. But I used to play wedding."

That night, Jessica took a twist-tie to bed and bent it back and forth to soften the paper. She tore it near the ends and crumpled the whole tie in her hand. She straightened it out again and then dropped it in her glass of water on her night table. Then she watched her digital clock, starting at 10:10, for five minutes, counting down the seconds, but counting much faster. When the clock reached 10:15, she had actually counted to 720. She lay the wet twist-tie flat to dry, sandwiched between two pieces of Kleenex. Tomorrow, when she wore the ring, Sarah would want to hold it, and Jessica would say no.

Draft Three

Dina Samuels was shorter than most of her students. She wore brown leather boots with heels that made her sound like a walking clock. When she arrived in a room, everyone looked up in surprise, expecting someone else. Bigger. Older.

Dina was wearing the boots when she went out for drinks with her friends after work. Robyn had a way of wearing statement jewellery — necklaces that fell just above her cleavage and rings that snaked up her fingers like silver vines. She straightened her hair into a shiny black bob that curved just below her jaw line. Dina always overslept, her hair thrown back into a loose bun so that it didn't irritate her face. Robyn had a job in a lab. She had a supervisor who was flying her to Bali for a conference. When Robyn left for the bathroom, Heather (who was studying to be a spin instructor) leaned over and said, "She wasn't even on the writing team for that paper. Everyone in her office hates her."

Dina said, "I heard this story today. I can't stop thinking about it."

Heather said, "Yeah?"

Robyn wasn't back, so Dina asked, "Do you think anyone would remember you twenty years from now just by your hands?"

Heather had dry cuticles. She was picking at them, but Dina noticed she stopped at the question.

"I dunno."

"I can't imagine," Dina said. "Meeting someone who looked at me like that."

"You will. We all will. Right?"

"This girl. Her grandparents met as kids during the war. And her grandmother—she literally saved this boy from starvation but no one knew. She brought him bread in the woods, every day. And then they met, almost twenty years later, on a blind date. And he remembered her hands. And they got engaged that night."

"That's crazy!"

Robyn pulled back her chair. "What's crazy?"

"Asking someone you just met to marry you," Heather said.

"No." Dina leaned forward. "That's not the point."

"Why? Who are you asking to marry?" Robyn lifted her wineglass toward the waiter, who nodded from across the room.

"I'm not. I'm just wondering if you can imagine having that kind of impact. That sort of connection."

Robyn said, "Sure." She reapplied her lipstick without a mirror. The colour of a fresh, deep cut.

"You don't get it," Dina said.

Robyn shrugged. "But I don't think you can determine the rest of your life, your happiness, after one evening—connection or no connection."

Dina stood up to leave. She was going to start crying and she never let herself cry in front of Robyn.

"I'm tired," she said, waving.

Robyn called out, "You're too sentimental!" but Dina was already by the door and her face was already wet.

Draft Four

Ava needed to believe in romance. There had to be something to look forward to. That, and she wanted to be Jessie's best friend. Jessie was pretty and thin. And the way she broke her ankle during the competition was just tragic enough that she looked lost, hobbling down the hall at school, in between classes. Her dance friends weren't offering to carry her books. Ava started with that offer, knowing that Jessie was too vulnerable to say no. Jessie wore real Ugg boots with black tights from Lululemon. Ava wore jeans that were too tight across her belly button, but she did not want to go shopping with her grandmother at Walmart. She had this feeling that carrying Jessie's books would change the way her clothes fit on her. Walking beside Jessie, she could imagine herself as someone who could lift her leg above her head.

The day Jessie told the story of her grandparents in Social Studies, Ava cried messy, fat tears and wiped her runny, disgusting nose. Love like that didn't exist in her family. Not from her mother, who hadn't sent a postcard, a text message, or even an Instagram post since leaving to figure things out in Las Vegas. Not from her grandmother, who always seemed to be frowning since Ava's grandfather died years ago. Certainly not from her older brother, Adam, who just stayed in his bedroom. If she did see him, he would yell at her, something like "Why are you always there?" What struck her most about Jessie's story was the immediacy and gentleness of the love. After class, Ava went over to Jessie's desk to gather her books. She was hiccupping and trying to breathe deeply. She said to Jessie, "Can I come over later and see the twist-tie?"

Jessie said, "Don't be stupid. It's not the real one. I just mentioned it. You know, for emphasis."

Some of the dance girls were crowding around now, leaning in to get Jessie's attention. But Jessie looked at Ava and cocked her head toward the door. Ava followed and felt them all watching her for once. Like she was finally on stage.

Ava was the one who told Jessie about the Valentine's Day contest from that talk show: "Tell Us the Greatest Love Story Never Told." That was how she finally got invited to Jessie's house. The girls sat on the floor in Jessie's bedroom, Jessie with Post-it Notes filled with details spread over a large piece of bristol board. On the top she wrote *Love Story* in purple marker, with a heart beside it like a period. Ava reached over and took the Post-it with the phrase *Park bench at night, kneeling in snow*. She said, "I think you should start with this one. Ms. Samuels always says you have to hook the audience."

Jessie sat with her bandaged leg elevated on a blue satin throw pillow. "Sarah is so stupid. She came up to me today with her silver medal from the comp on Saturday, and she was like, 'You can have this for the weekend, if you want.' And I was like, 'Yeah, last year? I got gold.' It's like, you're either my friend, or you're not my friend."

"Your grandfather's going to be famous when this story wins. Everyone will want to be your friend."

"I don't care. I don't think I want to dance anymore anyway."

"Someone might even make a movie about this, you know," Ava said. She sat up straighter. If she'd had a camera right then, she would have started filming. She would win an Oscar on her first try.

"Yeah!" Jessie sat up too. "I could totally play my grandmother. I so look like her. That's it, I want to do acting instead of dance. I don't care about Sarah, or any of them."

Ava stuck the Post-it she was still holding at the beginning of the line. The girls giggled while they mixed up all the details, wrote more Post-its of specifics they were missing, filling in the gaps. When they finally typed up the story on Jessie's iPad, they imagined that cute guy from Degrassi as the lovestruck lead. They couldn't even picture Zaida Sol on one knee in front of a park bench, shivering.

Draft Five

"Darling, stop."

Hillary's father never called her darling.

She said, "Excuse me?" They were sitting in the kitchen at her parents' old table. Her mother's absence was like a faded water stain. In the beginning she'd noticed it all the time. But she recognized that soon she wouldn't. There would be days when she sat at this table with her dad and Hillary would have to remind herself that her mother used to sit here too.

Sol reached across the table and put his hand on her arm.

"I feel like I'm drowning," she whispered.

"Don't say that."

"You never call me darling."

"Don't I?"

"That's like me calling you Father."

She watched her father fidget, unroll the sleeves of his button-down denim shirt, stand up to look for something without saying what.

"It's cold in here," he said.

"Daniel wants joint custody," Hillary answered. And then, "Dad, please sit."

Sol did and leaned in to cover Hillary's hand with his. "You knew that."

"I'm just tired, Dad. He knows I'm tired."

"Don't fight just to fight."

Hillary let out a long, loud whine. There were days when she could still trick herself into believing her father was a giant.

"Hil," he said. "I'm going to meet with that producer."

"Oh, Dad."

"It will be good for Jessie. And it's a good story. People should know."

Hillary closed her eyes and bowed her head forward,

resting her forehead on her folded hands on the table. Into the wood she whispered, "It's not real, Dad."

He reached over and lay his large palm, his puffy fingers on her head, massaging. Hillary had used mousse that morning so her hair had some body. She had given a presentation at work. She had read somewhere that limp hair made people look tired. Her hair felt stiff and sticky under her father's fingers, like she was coated in plastic.

"Every time I tell it, it's like your mother is right beside me."

Hillary turned her head so that she was looking at her father with one eye. "You never even called her darling."

He said, "Of course I did! Every day."

He wasn't a giant. He was shrinking and she hadn't the energy to change it or to question him. So what if he told this story, she asked herself. Who did it hurt for him to tell the world how much he loved his late wife?

Final Draft

Sol shook in the studio. His teeth chattered. It was only nerves, but worrying about his nerves made them worse. What if his teeth fell out while he was sitting there talking? Last night, Jessica had told him that Hillary wouldn't let her come downtown to watch.

THE GREATEST LOVE STORY NEVER TOLD

"But we're going to record it on our PVR. Ava and I are going to watch it after school. Maybe a whole group of kids from my class."

Ever since then, Sol felt as if his heart was sinking deep into his stomach, the ticking of it echoing in his bowels.

Sol waited backstage on a folding chair. No one around him had any white or grey hair. Blond, yes. The colour of sunrays behind thin, white clouds. The girls were in tank tops, short skirts with no tights, even in February. Hillary was forever trying to throw a sweater onto Jessie when she wore a tank top. Just last week Sol said, "Oh, leave her alone. She's not cold." But now he had the urge to drape everyone he saw in sweaters and blankets, to bring all these strangers around him, close, until he was entirely surrounded by their body heat and the air he breathed in was warm.

"Are you nervous?" the girl with the clipboard asked. She had tiny shoulders, toned like two tennis balls beneath her skin. She looked about ten years older than Jessie, same straight auburn hair, same narrow nose.

"Are you a dancer?" Sol asked.

Her face softened and she broke into a smile, her eyes bright like spotlights. "I am! I mean, I do some shows. You recognize me? I danced once with Cher when she was here. Drake too. I have an audition later today for a Mirvish production."

"Sure," Sol said. "I've seen you before."

"Awesome! That's amazing. I'm always telling my folks, you never know. You never know who you're gonna meet. They're so worried about me out here. 'Cause this is an internship and I'm constantly auditioning for stuff."

The girl touched his arm. "You're shaking! Oh, don't worry. She's a pussycat. She's gonna make you feel right at home. She's amazing when she talks to you. It's like there's no one else in the room."

He told her, "I don't know what to say."

"I'm going to get you a bottle of water or something. You just need to clear your mind."

"She was the most beautiful girl in the world," Sol said.

The clipboard girl was walking backwards away from him. "You stay there," she said. "I'll be right back."

"I don't know," he said, not loud enough for her to hear. From far away she really did look like Jessie, that look his granddaughter got just before she leapt across a stage, a deer about to bolt, anticipating.

The host had lovely wide lips, painted the same magenta as the stripe from Jessie's last dance costume and just as shiny. She smiled at Sol while she spoke, laughed at the end of her sentences, rocked back and forth in her seat to pat him on the wrist, to lean back with her hand on her chest whenever he said something touching.

"I have goosebumps," she said after he began telling her the story. He could barely hear the words coming out of his mouth for the sound of his heart beating in his head.

She broke in again. "Chills," she said and turned to her audience. "Don't you have chills?"

Well, of course they do, Sol thought. *It's freezing in here!* But he looked out at the audience of women nodding back at the host from their seats, some of them raising their arms as if from that far away she could see their hairs standing upright at attention.

The girl with the clipboard was off to the side, nodding too, smiling at Sol and giving him a thumbs-up. Sol smiled back and raised his thumb in response, which made everyone laugh and go "Aww." He didn't really get it — that they already loved him. That he didn't need to say a word more. The beauty of his story was not in the details but in the way he spoke about his Bella.

"She had lovely, tiny hands. I used to cover them with my own because she would get cold. And I remember what she wore on that first date. A red sweater. Like a heart. She was a walking valentine. I guess I knew that was a good sign."

The host let a tear fall down her cheek. Her makeup didn't run. Instead, Sol noticed how the teardrop carved a path through all the colour so that a thin line of her real skin showed through.

"Oh, darling," he said to her and handed her a tissue from the box on the coffee table between them.

"Now look. You've made me all verklempt!" she said, and then turned to her audience. "When we come back..."

She held Sol's hand, her fingernails digging into his palm. He didn't mind the sensation. It meant he was still here. The girl with the clipboard came over to lead him off the set and he said, "But I wasn't finished." Because he could sit there all day talking about his late wife, bringing her back with every word.

The Album

The Wedding, *Kabbalat Panim*

Alex went to her sister's wedding dressed like a boy. She and her father, Gary, danced like religious men, right down to the black hats and black suits. In a photo from the *kabbalat panim*, before the actual wedding ceremony, you couldn't even pick them out from the crowd surrounding the groom. The photographer stood on a chair and caught the shot from above looking down. The men danced the groom in to meet his bride, Ruchel, who sat in an oversized wicker chair, like some Alice in Wonderland garden throne. The shot had Ruchel in the background, clapping, surrounded by roses woven into the lattice. Alex was frozen in mid-jump, facing the groom, bouncing backwards to her sister, smiling like a cartoon kangaroo about to do something naughty. Gary looked up at Alex, face caught in surprise, like how could he have known

Ruchel's wedding would be like this? And even Alex transformed. Everywhere he looked, Gary was faced with something revolutionary.

Alex's suit was ill-fitting. So was Gary's. But then so was everyone's. Jackets either hung too loose or stretched too tight across shoulders. Black patent shoes scuffed at the toes from dancing at so many other weddings that summer. Beneath the jackets and the hats, they were all sweating already, their faces pale but with flushed cheeks. Their heavy glasses sliding down their noses. They were glassy-eyed from two-fisting the Scotch. The way they danced so close together as if to hold each other up, like dominoes just before they fall. Gary and Alex were the only ones who weren't plastered. Dancing right in front of Yehuda, the soon-to-be son/brother-in-law. Yehuda smiling past it all, to the top rim of the wicker throne, to the glimpses of Ruchel draped in taffeta and lace. This is the whirlwind of a three-month courtship. Of a nineteen-year-old bride, her twenty-one-year-old groom. Of their friends and family playing wedding, the favourite game of this season. Two kids preparing to play house when neither even knows how to use the washing machine.

Susan, Ruchel and Alex's mother, and Gary's wife, did not make it into the frame of this particular picture, even though she sat close to her daughter, the bride. But she was there, smiling through her misgivings, leaning in toward the action, wondering *doesn't everyone, ultimately, want to watch their children in moments of utter joy?* The wall of dancing men came toward them like a wave. Ruchel and Susan felt it like the final catch of breath before the water cascades over top. Alex beaming to be in the middle of all this. All these costumes and assignments. All these people so confident in their roles. Joy inspires confidence. Susan caught Gary's eye and then looked at their two children and wondered if she had ever seen them both so happy at the same time.

Susan's Dress

Alex took shot after iPhone shot of Susan in navy blue gowns, cocktail dresses, matching tops and skirts. Ruchel was in New Jersey with her soon-to-be in-laws, who were throwing a last-minute engagement party. Ruchel insisted Susan, Alex, and Gary did not need to attend. There wasn't much time and they had to find Susan a dress. Six weeks from engagement to *chuppah*. They had a lifetime to get to know Yehuda's family.

"Text me," Ruchel instructed. "From the shop. I want to see each dress you try on."

So Alex played messenger every time Susan emerged from the changing room. Ruchel fired back comments:
the hem can't fall above the knee
that one shows too much collarbone

she has to have her shoulders covered

this shouldn't be so hard!

tell her to buy the bolero jacket and have them stitch it to the straps so that it doesn't shift by accident

Alex edited every comment. "Rachel says that one looks great with the jacket. She likes the one with the higher neck. Can we go, Mum? Any of those look fine."

Susan didn't mind having to cover up. She'd had stomach cramps for weeks and bloating no matter what she ate. She hadn't told Alex or Ruchel yet, because she had to get through this wedding, like layers and layers of wrapping paper, before she could reveal to her kids, her husband, and herself, what was really going on. She knew better. She remembered how her father's body was shutting down at her own wedding. His arm trembling as he walked beside her. Really, she was the one walking him up the aisle as he dragged his foot behind him, as he limped and she said to him, "Hold on. I've got you."

Weddings have a wonderful way of monopolizing your life and pushing everything else to the side. So even when the doctor called and said, "I have the results from your ultrasound," Susan listened and then answered, "You know I can't deal with this until after Ruchel's wedding."

"You can't wait too long."

"Well then, thank God these religious kids are in such a rush!"

The navy blue satin shone and crinkled as Susan turned in front of the mirror. There was just enough beading along the collar so that the dress didn't look too heavy. The lace on the sleeves of the bolero jacket made her arms look slimmer. She told herself that at her age, she would have dressed like this anyway, even without all of Ruchel's religious rules. She wouldn't want her back arms jiggling on the dance floor, her flesh swaying off time with her clapping hands. She was not covering up. She was containing herself.

"Mum," Alex said again. "Can't I just tell her you're getting the spaghetti-strapped one and having the straps removed to make a tube top? Please? I want her to go ballistic at her stupid party."

Susan smiled and purposefully didn't answer. Alex never listened to her anyway. When they walked into the store, Susan had gently suggested that the shop carried a variety of styles for older *and* younger women. But Alex didn't even look up from the phone. *Let them poke at each other*, Susan thought now, like they used to in the back seat of her minivan. Let them nag and whine, hurling cyber insults while Ruchel drank kosher white wine from the Galilee region; while Alex fiddled with the iPhone, snapped photos before Susan could change her mind. "There," Alex said. "I'll give her two minutes. She'll panic but she won't cry."

"There's no reason to make her cry," Susan agreed, heading back into the change room. She suddenly needed to use the washroom urgently. Her face grew cold as she clenched her bowels, as she let the dress fall to the floor.

Susan heard the phone ding and then Alex laughing. "She's texting in all caps now. 'DIDN'T YOU SEE MY TEXTS???' Come on, Mum. Let me say 'What texts?' Let me tell her you're getting the outfit on a final sale. I'll tell her you look sexy."

Susan breathed through the cramps and thought, *At least they're talking.*

"One day you two will need each other," she managed. She didn't bother to do up her pants. She heard Alex snort in response.

As she rushed out toward the bathroom, Alex looked up from the phone and called after her, "Aviva thinks this is hysterical. She says I should dye my hair blue before the ceremony. Come on, Mum! To match your dress!"

Alex's Hair

Aviva put down the clippers and then snapped the photo on her smartphone. It was dramatic. Alex with a shaved head, long brown hair still tangled in the ponytail elastic now woven into the carpet of the bedroom floor. Number three all around, tapered at the bottom. Aviva had learned how to do the cut on YouTube. Alex looked like one of Ruchel's soon-to-be nephews in one of the pictures Ruchel was sharing on Facebook. The six- and seven-year-old boys crowding around her, squishing their faces into her frame. She'd used a selfie-stick for the reach, otherwise they wouldn't have all fit in.

Alex grabbed the phone and took a selfie, looking up in mock surprise, her eyes appearing even wider without all that hair.

"I'm posting this. I'm totally outing you," Aviva said.

Alex said, "Tag Rachel." Ruchel would be dress shopping, her phone vibrating in her purse. One of her almost-sisters-in-law grabbing it for her because Ruchel would be busy in the change room, being snapped from the base of her neck to her tailbone into a dress. A white lace suit of armour.

Rucheleh, the woman, with a name like Bracha or Perlie, might say. *Who's this?*

Alex imagined Ruchel's sinking heart, that look on her face when she came out of the change room, her tight lips, her mouth open with a million suggestions ready on her tongue. And then the picture, flashed up on the screen; you could practically hear Alex laughing, as if pointing right at her sister. Aviva had created the hashtag #meetwilliam.

My cousin, Ruchel would offer. Because there was never a point in denying their resemblance. Even without Alex's hair. *He has strange friends.*

Aviva stepped toward Alex. Alex watched her bare feet nestle amongst the hair, her toes curling and flexing, gathering the strands into piles. Aviva was taller than Alex by half a head, even without the boots. That year she'd gone off meat and her lips had a grey tinge because of it. Alex reached up to trace them. They were dry and puckered like dates.

Aviva's hand brushed over Alex's fuzzy skull. Alex could feel the stunted hairs shifting under her fingers. Aviva murmured, "I like Will. Will is sexy."

Mother and Daughters

Ruchel sat on her mother's living room couch, Alex on one side, Susan on the other. This picture would be best captured from the upstairs landing that looked over the living room/dining room, a feature unique to this model of house in Thornhill, with the sloping ceiling, the wooden railing like an indoor balcony. Susan imagined how a photographer perched up there would be at enough of a distance to capture the proud mother with her two girls, Ruchel swiping through pictures on her iPad, reviewing dresses she was considering having them wear for the upcoming ceremony. If snapped at just the right moment, the photo would show Susan and Alex looking over Ruchel's shoulder, just before Alex drew a face of disgust, or Susan's eye widened in exaggerated support when Ruchel looked up at her, pleading. One of those digital SLR cameras could click through a series of shots, capturing just the right moment when all three focused on the same thing, at the same time, before their individual needs tore their attention apart. If she'd realized, Susan would have had Gary stay home from the office that day. He was always good at getting the girls to stand together, even when they were like magnets pushing each other apart.

Alex hadn't yet cut her hair. She wore it in a low ponytail. It was oily at the scalp and needed a wash. She wore her Montreal Canadiens Price jersey. Loose jeans torn at the knee. She was picking at the threads from the tear when she snorted and said, "Like hell I'm wearing a dress."

Ruchel didn't react. She continued to swipe through the pictures methodically. She'd known Alex would say that. "You don't always have a choice. It's an Orthodox *shul*. This is what women do."

Alex folded her arms. Ruchel may not have been looking up, but Susan was. Susan caught the smirk spreading across Alex's face. She said, "Don't."

Alex said, "Fuck, Rachel already knows."

Ruchel looked up then. "Please don't swear. I'm not going to sit here if you insist on being filthy."

Alex laughed, but Susan reached behind Ruchel and placed her hand on Alex's shoulder, tilted her head, pleading. Alex would have continued, but she had made a promise to her mother that she would behave. So she tucked her lips tight around her teeth, widened her eyes at her mother, and yelled all the profanities she wanted to inside her head.

"We're going with silver, for the gowns," Ruchel continued. "The nieces will wear their cream dresses with silver sashes. Ages ago, Yehuda's sisters bought these dresses—here, these ones—in all kinds of sizes. So now whenever there's a wedding, they just choose a different colour ribbon. It's brilliant. Last year there were four weddings in his family."

"The expense alone!" Susan said. She knew a religious family, their neighbours, where the son got married, had a baby, and was divorced all before he turned twenty-two. The ex-daughter-in-law was originally from Australia. Someone told Susan she'd left with the baby girl for Israel. Now the boy sat in his parents' backyard, smoking up in the middle of the day. Didn't they meet and get engaged all in one summer? Didn't Ruchel even comment when they got divorced, "Oh, yeah. They rushed into things."

"What's the rush?" Gary had pleaded when Ruchel and Yehuda called from New Jersey, three weeks before, to tell them about their engagement. It was the same question they'd asked Alex two months earlier when she said she was ready to transition. The same question Susan had whispered on the phone to her doctor earlier today, when she got the call about the results.

"This has to be dealt with soon," the doctor insisted. "We don't know how aggressive this can become."

And now, it seemed to Susan, each of them was facing a change that they were powerless to stop. So this moment on the couch was their last chance to sit together, mother and daughters, as polarized as they'd always been. But at least they were together, here. Alex had told her earlier that she was thinking of changing her name. She liked "William." There was nothing ambiguous about it. She said she didn't want anyone questioning who she really was.

Ruchel had recently mentioned a friend whose sister was seriously ill. The sister had changed her name to try to fool the Evil Eye into handing her back her health. Susan had been considering a new name too. She'd always thought her name sounded meek. She wanted to be called something like Blaise, or Bryna. Something with a B, so that you have to use all the muscles in your mouth to pronounce it. Something that commanded effort.

"I've been thinking," she told the girls, "about how you've both changed but stayed the same. How some things will be different moving forward but some things won't. You know? We're all learning to accept who we are."

Alex snorted again. Ruchel rolled her eyes. She said, "I can't tell anyone about Alex. No one I'm friends with would understand."

"My friends can't stand you either!"

Susan's arm was still stretched out, touching both her daughters from behind. They didn't realize, but they both inched toward her on the couch, toward the hollow of her side and underarm. She thought, *This shot. Right here.* It's the energy of all that tension just before everyone disperses, spinning off in all directions.

Keeping Ghosts Warm

SHULA WAS MEETING her father at a Chinese restaurant in downtown Toronto at lunchtime. She wore her wig. She wouldn't eat a thing off the *treif* dishes, but she ordered a jasmine tea while waiting for him. Even still, she sipped it with the cup barely touching her lips, with her fingers so tense her knuckles cracked as she set the cup back down on the table. The restaurant smelled like crisp, sweet pork fat. A young couple sat at the table beside her, arguing by not saying a word. The girl stabbed at her noodles with her chopsticks.

Shula's father was fifteen minutes late. A flat-screen TV on the wall beside the cashier showed a video of a Chinese girl band, each member wearing a wig cut in a thick bob in different colours — pink, purple, and daffodil yellow. The sound was turned down so that everyone could hear the Christmas carols from the CD player on the counter. Shula watched the girls' wide eyes, lips like candy *O*s, mouthing their Mandarin song out of sync to "God Rest Ye Merry Gentlemen."

"You wearing this costume all the time now?" Her father pulled at the chair opposite her and it squeaked across the floor. His face was different shades of grey, the skin hanging as if too heavy for the muscle and bones of his forehead, his jaw. His teeth reminded Shula of pebbles on a beach at the end of a hot day, dried by the unfiltered sun.

She didn't reply before he asked, "You ordered?"

"I'm not eating," she told him.

"C'mon, Janis."

"Don't."

"Then what the hell are we doing here?"

"What do you want, Dad?"

Shula looked up at the waitress behind the counter, who was straightening a pile of takeout menus. Her father waved and the girl came over to them.

"I want your egg rolls. And those crispy noodles with the fried pork. The crunchy ones. Bring two plates," her father said.

When she left, Shula said, "I told you I'm not eating." Her father looked down at the table and folded his napkin like a fan. He looked up and then out the window, still playing with the paper.

"There's stuff at the house that's yours. I need you to go through it. I have to sell."

"Whatever I have there, you can just throw out."

"I know," her father said, flattening out the wrinkled napkin as if he were kneading dough. He put it on his lap and then looked up at Shula. "It's so easy for you to throw things away."

"You have my permission."

"I don't want your goddamn permission. I shouldn't have to move your junk. I have enough junk of my own."

"There are companies now who will do that for you."

"I'm not spending money like water. And don't tell me he's offering."

Shula said nothing about her husband. She drank her tea, this time with the ceramic firmly against her mouth.

"Where are you going to live?" she asked.

"A condo. Don't worry. Nowhere close to you."

Shula looked down at the table, at the chopsticks crossed like legs above her plate. "I don't know when I can get out there."

"I need you to go this weekend. Because of the agent. Clear your things. I'm staying with Barbara. She's having everyone for dinner on Sunday. They ask about you. I say I don't know how the hell you are."

The waitress brought his food and the extra plate, which stayed empty. He cut the egg roll lengthwise and poured plum sauce into the wound. It steamed and Shula felt her stomach contracting.

"I don't know if I can get away this weekend."

"Tell that husband of yours that I said so."

. . .

TWO WEEKS EARLIER AHARON had heard his parents
fighting. Something about California. He heard his
father's laptop thud against the wall. He ran into their
room and found his father bent over the broken computer. His mother's hands reminded him of bat wings,
fingers spread like those tiny bones just before the bat
takes off. His father looked up at him and then said,
"For God's sake, Shula." Aharon watched as his father
nudged the computer with his foot. Bent down to push
the drywall dust into a pile.

Aharon went back into his bedroom and looked out
the window. A white and grey cat, thick body, stumpy
legs, walked along the sidewalk across the street. He
watched until he couldn't see it anymore. In the distance he saw the lights from Bathurst Street, the cars on
the main road heading toward the highway, the parking
lot for the strip mall with the dentist. California was
west of all of that.

Shula came into Aharon's room and sat on the edge
of his bed. She had not taken off her wig yet and it
shone beneath the pot lights in his room, a golden
ring reflected off the shiny strands. Just past her, on his
bookshelf, was a photo of the three of them taken last

year in honour of his bar mitzvah, Aharon in the black-and-white prayer shawl that had been his father's when he was thirteen. His mother had had her makeup done for the photos, and her eyes looked wider than normal. She had on long fake eyelashes, curled, and they made her look surprised that God had blessed them with this *simcha*. His father wore a tall black hat that created a shadow over his face. The photographer kept telling him to lean away from Aharon, because of the shadow. And only now did Aharon realize that it looked like his father was stepping away.

Shula said, "Did you know about her?"

She didn't turn around to look at him. Aharon wasn't sure if she was speaking to him. After a moment he said, "No, Ima." He could hear his dad lugging a suitcase up the stairs, the wheels bumping each step like a hiccup.

Shula rubbed her hands together and they turned red from the friction. Aharon said, "She's in California?" But it came out as a whisper. Shula turned around and placed one of her red hands on top of his leg. She tried to smile but her chin quivered. She said, "I told him you don't leave the ones you love."

Aharon moved his leg away from her hand. Her face was falling. It looked like someone was draining her from behind. Like she would soon collapse in a deflated heap across his bed. He sat up straighter and said, "You shouldn't have yelled at him."

"This was a long time coming."

"You yell too much. You're always angry."

Shula said, "We stick together," but even those words came out light, barely audible. Shula looked at the door.

Aharon could hear his father emptying his drawers, the hangers in the closet clanging together as he removed his shirts, his suit jackets.

Shula got up then and left the room. She walked slowly, as if her legs were aching. Aharon willed himself to hate her. He wanted to spit. But instead he turned over and lay face down on his mattress, the pillow over his head, holding it tight by his ears. He lay like that so that he didn't hear his father packing his car, backing it out of the driveway, heading west to Bathurst, the 407 highway, Windsor, Detroit, Chicago, California.

NOW, TWO WEEKS LATER, he heard his mother backing out of the driveway late at night, tires crunching over dry snow. He wondered if she was finally chasing after his father. It was one in the morning. In his dark bedroom, where he was supposed to be asleep, Aharon was writing a screenplay on his laptop, a scene where his main character, a cross between an elf and a wizard and a hobbit, discovers that his parents are not dead after all but are waiting for him to rescue them. When he could no longer hear his mother's car driving away, he opened up the last email from his father, which said, "Don't come yet," and he blinked, trying to change the letters.

When he came home from school that day, his mother had been sitting in the kitchen without her wig. Her natural hair was frizzy, the colour of weathered wood, gathered at the nape of her neck in a ponytail, strands escaping all around her head like an unfocused photograph. She stared at the centre of the table as if a scene were playing out in front of her.

"Ima?" he'd said. It was close to suppertime and the house smelled like nothing.

Shula had turned her head swiftly. She opened her mouth to speak, but then her jaw just hung there. Aharon turned the lights on, opened the fridge for even more light. He wished he had a spotlight to shine on her face and make her blink.

She finally said, "Something's come up. I have to go to Hamilton."

"Okay."

"Probably Sunday. It's nothing serious."

"What's in Hamilton?"

"Just something I have to pick up."

Aharon poured himself orange juice, grabbed a handful of cold potato wedges.

"I might go sooner," she said. But she still didn't move. He hated that she was asking him for permission. He slammed the fridge door closed. He hated that in the last two weeks since his father left, she had done nothing without checking with him first.

"I don't give a fuck," he said, knowing full well it was an *avera*, a sin, to talk to his mother like that. But he didn't care. And she didn't bother to tell him to watch his mouth.

AHARON GOT OUT OF BED and shivered. He shuffled barefoot to his parents' room, where his mother's bed was still made, where on her dresser sat her wig atop the faceless Styrofoam head. Aharon put it on and smelled her—coffee and cocoa butter. He saw himself in her full-length mirror—bulging knees and elbows, rounded shoulders folding into his chest. His jaw had recently grown wider; his oily nose and chin were full of black-heads. But he didn't pay attention to that. Instead, he recognized his mother's cheekbones on his face, high-lighted by the layers cut into the wig. In the light, the wig was the colour of cola, though he'd heard his moth-er's friends describe it like coffee: "mocha," "espresso." She hadn't yelled at all since his father left. The house was so terrifyingly quiet he felt as if he were on a TV show with the sound off.

• • •

IN THE CAR DRIVING to Hamilton, Shula played Christmas carols on the radio and sang along, paus-ing when Jesus was mentioned. In between "Joy to the World" and "Little Drummer Boy," she reached into her purse for an apple and said the blessing on fruit from a tree before biting into it. Her eyes burned from exhaustion, her neck was sweaty. She'd thought Aharon was asleep, so she left him a sticky note on the mirror in his bathroom that said, *Decided to go now. Will be back soon. Eat oatmeal for breakfast. Cold outside.*

Shula's key stuck in the front door lock and for a moment she worried that her father had had them changed in the last fifteen years. She jiggled the key and then finally the bolt clicked. Her driving gloves did little to keep her fingers warm, and she blew on her hands as she walked inside. The power was out in the house. Shula went down to the basement in her boots and coat to find the fuse box. She found a flashlight on her father's workbench and when she turned it on, the light beamed around the thick darkness like the beam from a lighthouse through Atlantic fog. The basement stank of old water damage, mouldy carpet, wet pavement. The light landed on the table with her father's unfinished model railroad diorama. A skeleton of a mountain, shaped out of chicken wire, was only half-plastered in papier mâché newspaper, layers of obituaries and classified ads in criss-crossed strips. The plywood board below was covered in mossy green foam that crumbled beneath Shula's fingers as she leaned in to look. There were some buildings — a station, a hotel — but with the unfinished landscape, it just looked as if her father had tried to build the town backwards. The track was black from oxidization—at first she wondered if this was deliberate, but no. It was just the only way this photograph had aged over time.

Her father had been inspired by a summer trip to Cape Breton, Nova Scotia, where they toured an enormous model railroad built by a man named John. Shula remembered John's swollen belly, the way he had to bend down at his knees and then over the tracks so that he didn't knock any of the minute scenery over with his girth. Shula was twelve years old then and only agreed to go see the railroad because her knees hurt from sitting scrunched up in the back seat of the car for two days. Her mother did not get out. She rolled down her window and lit a cigarette, the smoke rising toward the sky in a thin line, like the chain from a light bulb in a basement.

Shula had no idea John's model railroad would be beautiful. There were snow-capped mountains and a summer beachside. A town with a fairground, a station, and a drive-in movie theatre. John turned the lights down in the room so that they could see the lights inside all the buildings.

"It looks like they're moving," Shula said about the people sitting in the diner.

"I know," said John. "It's like playing God."

Shula's dad bent down so that his eyes were at track level. John ran a train right by his nose, the headlight coming out of the tunnel, shining a spot on his forehead and then rushing past. Her dad didn't blink, but Shula jumped back, preferring to remain a few feet from the low tabletop, viewing everything from a distance.

John ran a small shop at the front of his building. Shula's father piled supplies on the counter—track and trees, kits for buildings, miniature people frozen in mid-step, parents holding hands with their children. Shula found a necklace on a rack, a pewter seashell hidden amongst colouring books and train whistles. She slipped it onto the counter. Her father didn't even notice. John winked at her and put the necklace into a paper bag and motioned for her to take it, which she did while her father was busy counting packs of track. She wasn't stealing, but the deception made her stomach tingle, right up to the moment later, in the car, when her mother eyed the paper bag and said, "What did you get?"

Shula answered, "A necklace. With my own money."

Her dad looked at her and then back at the road, but Shula saw the look on his face. That moment where his eyebrows knit together, when he realized he couldn't remember her paying for anything. But maybe it was more than that—it was her father realizing that she had been there with him all along and he hadn't even noticed.

NOW, IN THE DARK BASEMENT, Shula stepped back from the diorama, so that the light from the flashlight widened like an unfolding curtain. She spotted the miniature billboard to the side of the mountain advertising Janis's Diner. At the other end of the tracks was the hotel, thin with curved windows, like from a western, called Gail's Place, named after her mother. Shula remembered sitting on a stool (it was still there, beside the diorama, steel legs, red leatherette seat) while her father sat hunched over the tracks, fumbling over the small parts with his wide fingers, sighing and blowing puffs of green up from the fake grass to his upper lips and cheeks. Shula walked forward, following the light skating on the tracks. She leaned over the table, put her nose close to the tracks, peeked into the papier mâché mountain tunnel and waited for a train, which was not coming.

. . .

AHARON TUCKED A STRAND of his mother's hair behind his ear. It felt like the satin sash of his mother's dressing gown that he used to play with when she read to him in bed. He curled the strand of hair the way he used to weave the sash around his fingers. The whole house was cast in blue light, shadows criss-crossing each other from the living room to the dining room to the hallway. Outside, the light from the street lamps and from the house lights his father had installed two months ago flickered and reflected off the snow. Light adding to light adding to light, almost brighter than the sun. Aharon turned away from the window and squinted his eyes to adjust back to the shadows.

He did not make oatmeal. Instead, he found smoked turkey breast in the fridge and cheddar cheese and some leftover braided challah. He double-wrapped his sandwich in tinfoil and turned on the oven. While the cheese melted into the creases of the turkey cut, Aharon had a rabbinic argument with himself about whether or not turkey is really meat, about how it's never explicitly mentioned in the Torah; how, technically, there is nothing in Jewish law to preclude him from having the sandwich that was currently *treifing* up his mother's oven. The rabbis in his head yelled and screamed over ancient text, pages open like mounds of Hebrew letters, and Aharon lost track of the arguments, the pages, the reasons why he wrapped the stupid sandwich in the first place. Somewhere between the thickness of the tinfoil and the exact ratio of cheese to questionable meat, he put his head down on the kitchen table and wept. The table was from a metal patio set. There was a hole in the centre for an umbrella. The top felt cool against his forehead. His mother's hair fell along his cheeks like a whisper.

. . .

SHULA WAS ALSO IN HER childhood kitchen. She had finished with the fuse box and could now make coffee. She wrapped her hands around the coffee pot and the heat travelled up her arms to her face, to the tip of her freezing nose. Her fingers tingled from thawing and she wiggled her toes in her boots until she could feel them moving. Her father had the heat turned all the way down. He used to say, "No sense keeping the ghosts warm." It didn't even occur to Shula to turn it up. She could feel the kitchen floor even through the soles of her boots, like a skating rink. The cupboard doors above her didn't close properly. Over time, the house had shifted one way, so now they didn't properly align. It made everything look off, like a funhouse, like Shula should hold her head at an angle just to see the room straight.

The house still smelled of her mother. Her mother had smoked and smoked until the smoke travelled up to her brain and settled there like a cloud, growing heavy, pushing every other part of her mind aside. In the end, when she breathed through her nose, her breath came out grey. Shula used to smell cigarettes even when she was sleeping.

That smell was the first thing she'd noticed the night she and Avi came back to announce their engagement. Her father had answered the door and said, "Like hell you will," and Shula took a step back. She wasn't knocked over by his defiance. It was the stench of the house, the feeling that when they walked in, the smoke would rob them of their breath. Avi also stepped back. As Shula pushed past her father, she heard him say to Avi, "You're not welcome in here."

Shula was twenty-one and had recently decided to change her name from Janis; also that her parents' secular take on Jewish life did not mesh with her blossoming fear of God. She pushed past her father to find her mother lying in her bed, covered in blankets, so many and so thick, but her fingers were still cold when Shula grabbed her hand to wake her.

"Mum," she said, "I want you to see." She pressed her new ring into her mother's palm, the white gold and the diamond bright like fire.

Her mother shifting and moaning while her father yelled from the front hall, "Does he even know your real name?"

"Mum, look."

Shula's mother lifted her head, breathed out a grey sigh from her nose and handed back the ring.

"Get me one." She pointed at her dresser.

And so Shula slipped the ring back on, felt the diamond fall toward her pinky because the band would need to be sized. Took a cigarette out for her mother and lit it with the neon green Bic lighter. She held it between her thumb and forefinger. When she put it to her mother's parched lips, she held her other hand beneath it to catch the ash. It burned like hot snowflakes.

"Go," her mother said after a while. "Don't wait for me."

"We're thinking in the spring."

"That's not for me."

"It would be nice," Shula said.

"You know I won't be there." Every word her mother said was like ice melting, there and then gone.

"We wanted you to know."

"You've only wanted for yourself for the last three years."

Shula got up and backed away, her ring now completely turned around on her finger so that she saw only the plain band. Her dad was in the kitchen when she opened the front door to leave.

"I'm not paying for that kind of wedding," he said. Avi was in the car and Shula could hear the nasally Israeli religious music, the car engine humming, her fiancé taking off the parking brake, ready to go.

. . .

WHEN SHE OPENED THE door to her bedroom, she felt air. The door didn't quite squeak so much as sigh. Her T-shirts were still folded in her dresser drawer, white gloss paint, white ceramic knobs. Pictures of her friends from high school were still stuck into the sides of her vanity mirror. One had fallen off, sometime between then and now, a photo of a group of girls in baggy sweaters, oversized smiles, their faces lying on the table, smiling up at the ceiling.

Shula put everything into garbage bags, the photos, the empty perfume bottles, the lipstick that smelled like old woman. And then all her clothes, her faded underwear, her creased T-shirts, those baggy sweaters. She worked around the room, taking down posters, dumping shoe boxes from the closet, closing one garbage bag and then opening another for the stuffed animals on her bed, the CDs stacked against the wall, the paperback novels of high-school girls building up to that kiss, the spines bent to that page. She went so far as to strip the bed, stuffing down her comforter and sheets, smelling her adolescent self, asleep, the stale scent of spearmint, french fries, and nail polish all locked in that bedding and released one last time before she closed the bag.

She considered saving something to bring home to Aharon, but only after she had filled all the bags. And she didn't want to risk opening the bags, spilling the contents out all over the floor, being faced with a jumbled pile of what she used to be.

She remembered visiting a tarot card reader with her girlfriends, after graduation. The smell of lilac and incense, a tapestry on the wall behind the woman with oily wrinkles around her mouth. The purple elephant on the tapestry decorated in small, rounded mirrors, reflecting the candlelight from the red votive candle on the table. And the woman saying, "There is a boy, running. And you are behind him."

Shula thought about going home to Aharon. That maybe yes, she should bring the bags. About how she would wake him and they would make a bonfire in the backyard. Aharon would carry the wood from the side of the house and she would marvel at his muscles, the hints of adulthood, the way he built the fire for her, piled it with her things, and then stoked it to make sure everything had burned away. And they would sit together, the contrast between the heat from the fire and the cold wind on their necks. They would both close their eyes and breathe deeply.

· · ·

AHARON STARED AT HIS FEET, listening to the phone ring in California, his father's cell. When his dad answered, Aharon heard conversation, laughter, pockets of music like bubbles floating in and out of the static.

"Aharon? You already up?"

"Yeah."

"This early?"

"It's too quiet."

"I can't hear you."

"I'm ready to come, Abba."

"I'm walking somewhere quieter. Hold on."

"I'm ready. I'm going to book the ticket. I can't stay here anymore."

"Hold on, Aharon."

"She's not even here."

There was muffling on the other end of the phone, the cracks and scratches of the mouthpiece being smothered, of voices.

"Aharon? You there? Okay. Listen. I'm working things out. Naama wants you to come. Really. I want you. But now's not the time. It's too soon. We have to let everything settle. You know, I'm just starting my teaching. It's a great yeshiva, but I need time. And your mother needs you. You know she's not going to let you go right now. Not to me, like this. But be patient, *boychuk*. I've got it."

"Okay."

Aharon's tears dripped on either side of his feet, splashed on the kitchen tile. When the line went silent, he squinted and imagined the tiny puddles like lights blinking at him.

He hung up the phone and went to pack his bag, sniffing back the drips of snot running out of his nose. He used a green duffle bag from the women's gym his mother had joined once for three months. Her towel was still in there and he tossed it hard to the floor of the landing outside his room. Aharon grabbed his T-shirts, gym shorts, sports sandals that were too small but would do for now. No socks (he'd only wear sandals in

California, all the time). Underwear. *Tzitzit.* He would write her a note too. Leave it on her bathroom mirror. Something like, *Not coming back. Eat whatever the hell you want.* He thought of taking her wig with him. Of how she would come looking for him with her bare head, her frizzy, worn-out brown hair sticking out everywhere like stuffing from an old couch.

. . .

SHULA FILLED THE BACK seat of her car with her old life. The bags were heavier than she'd thought they would be. Or she was just tired. Or the weight of it all—this final visit, those mementos like puzzle pieces that, put together, might have built a shadow of what she once was—was not exactly lifted yet. And part of her wanted to curl up right there, on top of those garbage bags in the back of her car and fall asleep surrounded by it all one last time. But instead she locked the house, took the key off her ring, and dropped it in the grate at the end of the driveway.

THE WINTER AFTER THE family trip to the Maritimes, she had lost her shell necklace down that grate. Her mother had made her put on a scarf on their way to a holiday concert, and the wool itched her neck like mosquitoes pricking. She tugged at it while she waited for her mother to come out and unlock the car. Her necklace must have fallen off and slipped through the slots of the grate. She didn't notice at the time. She was only relieved by the cool air on her sweaty neck, opening her jacket against the winter night.

"It's not so cold," she said to her mother, who shook her head as they climbed into the car, as the vents blew out cold air and Shula didn't complain. She used to play with the silver seashell pendant, put it in her mouth and run her tongue along the ridges, suck on the sharp, sour metal, the tingle that ran all around the inside of her lips. When she wore it, she thought of how she had been invisible, how one day she would grow up, move away, and slip into another life when neither of her parents were really looking. She lifted her fingers and felt her bare collarbone, the shock of her warm skin brushed by cold fingers.

"Oh," she said, as if only just then hearing the necklace ping against the metal grate. She heard the echo of the fall too. The drip as it landed in the water below, the gulp as it was swallowed down the pipes with the drenched brown leaves, the thin yellow grass.

"What?" her mother asked. She was squinting out the window, looking for parking. They drove by a building with a display of the three wise men on horseback. Shula noticed one of the horses was missing an eye.

"Nothing," she said, but she felt her throat tighten. Her mother sighed because all the cheap lots were full. "I forgot my necklace."

"I told you not to rush."

Shula did up her jacket and wrapped the scarf around her neck. She itched for the rest of the night.

· · ·

IT'S SO EASY TO LEAVE, Aharon thought as he stood outside, waiting for his Uber. He was still wearing Shula's wig. No hat. The wind lifted up the hair and blew it off his shoulders. It fell back against his neck like a curtain blowing open and then closed. It was six in the morning. The sky was still as dark as in the middle of the night. There wasn't even light around the edges yet. He wore his winter coat, which he planned to throw out when he got to the airport, along with the wig. He imagined shedding himself when he got there, the way a snake discards its old skin. And how far would he go? His coat, the wig. Perhaps his *kippah,* which he always had clipped to his head when he was out. He could feel it in his jacket pocket, a tight crocheted disk with the Toronto Blue Jays logo woven in. Or his *tzitzit,* the fringes he wore under his shirts to remind him of God's presence in the four corners of the Earth. The way they would brush against his leg when he walked, a reminder like a ribbon around a finger. Don't forget all those commandments. Even the one that says *kabed et avicha v'et eemecha* — honour thy father and thy mother. He didn't know how much he would shed. He didn't know, he didn't know — and he jumped up and down both to keep warm and to stamp the ground like a child having a silent tantrum because he didn't know if, when he got there, he would rip them off from under his shirt, pull them up through his collar and over his head, stuff them into a ball so that the fringes were all tangled and meaningless and hidden. He didn't know if he could do it, and whether he would feel naked standing there. As if everyone would be looking at him, even though he was really trying to be invisible.

His next-door neighbour, Mrs. Levine, came out of her house to take the garbage and recycling to the curb. Her grandchildren lived with her because their mother had run off a few years ago. Shula had said recently that Aharon should try to be friends with the boy. *And now,* Aharon thought, *we have this in common. Maybe there is something about this street. A reason why nobody stays.* As soon as he heard Mrs. Levine coming, he took the wig off his head, stuffed it in his pocket. His head immediately felt cold and he was beginning to get a headache from not sleeping, from the wind that pricked his forehead and ears.

Mrs. Levine said, "Oh!" when she saw him waiting on the curb. "You're up early."

"Basketball practice," Aharon answered. "I'm getting a ride."

"Nice of you to let your mum sleep."

"Yeah."

She steadied her green bin, which wobbled down the incline, and then she turned back to Aharon. "You really should be in a hat. With these kinds of temperatures, you lose all your body heat from the top of your head."

Aharon nodded and looked at the ground. He could feel it—the heat escaping from his cold, frozen head.

Mrs. Levine shook her covered head as she walked away to get her mail from her locked cubby in the community mailbox across the street.

When the car pulled up, Aharon stepped back from the curb. The driver rolled down the window and called out, "You going to the airport?" Aharon kept going, backing away toward the house—maybe this wasn't so easy. Maybe there was an invisible rope that someone was pulling, like a mime, all their muscles tense, grabbing and grabbing at that rope attached to him, and even when he tried to move forward, he kept going back. The driver wore a Blue Jays baseball cap. He called out even louder, "You getting in?" Mrs. Levine was watching from across the road. She had her mouth open as Aharon picked up his bag and held it firm over his shoulder. She was yelling, "Wait!" as he got in and said to the driver, "I'm late for my flight."

WHEN SHULA GOT HOME, Mrs. Levine was pounding on her front door. Shula's eyes stung from not sleeping, her fingers ached because her gloves just weren't warm enough. She pulled into her driveway as the light was starting to rise from the horizon, pink streaks across the sky. She remembered her father saying, "Red sky at morning, sailors take warning."

Mrs. Levine was by her car door before Shula got out. She was crying. She was saying, "You just missed him! I tried to stop him. He took a taxi. Kids don't take taxis to basketball."

Shula got out and ran into the middle of the empty street. She looked up and down in both directions. Down the block someone got into their car and closed the door, started the engine. Mrs. Levine pleaded from behind her, "You have to go after him. You can't just let him go. I know about this kind of thing!"

Shula stood with her arms out, as if Aharon were running back down the middle of the street, a gummy toddler, flinging himself into her arms only to scramble down again and run away laughing. A chasing game, where she was always it.

The Last Man Standing

You know, rabbi, my sister would never believe that I'm sitting here with you. She's smart. Much smarter than I'll ever be. She is the kind of person who can look at someone and size them up right away. She always pegs them bang on.

She told me, before she left for Israel, she said to me at the airport, "Sometimes I feel like I'm constantly holding your hand so that you don't run into traffic."

I snorted. Because I'm older than she is by two years.

Her eyes got all watery. She said, "The only reason I don't want to go is because I'm afraid for you."

I looked away from her. It felt like she was cutting at me with a thousand knives. I said, "Shut up. I'm not your fucking kid."

She was off to Israel to join the army. A lone soldier. For a long time after she left, even now, I think of her standing in a desert, an Uzi diagonal across her back.

That green khaki uniform. Blowing sand. Like she's protecting that whole country, alone.

She put her knapsack over her shoulder and turned away from me into the security line. She said, "Just don't let yourself become an asshole."

I am an asshole. When we were kids, living with our grandmother, she would try too hard to be good, and I was always making fun of her. I hated how she vacuumed every night without being asked. How my grandmother would head upstairs with a sigh and a "thank you." But what I hated the most was the stupid grin on Ava's face, like she'd been granted one more night's stay. I wanted to yell at her—*Our mother left, she wasn't kicked out!* But instead I would make faces, or spill potato chip crumbs. Because I knew we were there for good. We were the ones who should have said thank you every night.

Ava never asked about our dad. My grandmother had a family photo on the wall from before Ava was born but when I was a baby. I'm in my mother's arms and reaching out sideways away from the group. Someone was standing beside her, but had been cut out from the picture. There's a wavy edge, but the photo is still in a frame, so it's like all of us—my grandparents, me, my mum, some cousins, and this ghost—captured in a pewter box. That was all I ever had to go by. My father was just a gap.

Here's what I know now:

1. His name is Dmitry. But he went by many nicknames.
2. He used to divide his time between Toronto and Moscow.
3. He had a chain of nightclubs at one point.

I found stuff about him in Russian online. Google translated the most recent article into something like "Cherry Man Giant Bread Lost." So I think he lost it all, whatever he had. He looks ghostly in his picture, deep pockets under his eyes. Long face. Shiny bald head. And now that's the shadow I fit into the photograph in my memory, the person I was reaching for.

I bet you're wishing they'd assigned you someone else. Maybe someone with a gambling addiction. Or a kid whose mother's afraid he's addicted to weed. I bet you didn't become a rabbi to deal with my kind of shit. I have to unload it all before I can rebuild. That's why they call it rehabilitation, right? Re-Ha-Build.

I would like to visit her, my sister, Ava. In Israel. I don't know if they'll even let me travel. But maybe that's something you can do after we're done together. Vouch for me. I'd really like to see her. If I'm standing in front of her, she'll have to look at my face. And I know her. I know that as much as she's been spitting at me in her head for years, she couldn't bring herself to do it for real. I'll tell her I've come all this way to take her for coffee. I even know about Aroma. That Israeli Starbucks. I'll take her there and buy her a croissant and a latte. I'll tell her it's a start.

She can't blame me for being angry. I should blame her for shrugging it all off. Some asshole plows down our grandmother — while she was buying a dozen fucking bagels — and Ava doesn't even come in for the funeral. I don't even think she asked for the leave. On the phone she was crying to me. I remember her like, "I'm so alone here. You don't know how hard it is to be away." I was like, Are you fucking kidding me? You know what? You bury our grandmother by yourself, stand at her fucking grave with her crazy brother and a handful of friends behind you. And of course it's raining. So you dig at that mound of dirt, shovel after shovel of mud onto her coffin and you don't leave until she's completely covered. You're soaking wet and your hands are twisted and frozen, and everyone's telling you it's enough. But you're like, "No fucking way." And so you keep standing there in the rain while they all leave. Even crazy Uncle Isaac, who goes to watch you from your car because you're his only ride. And when you finally get in and you're shivering so hard you can't hold your fucking car keys, and he says to you, "If that bastard was here right now, I'd tell you to plow him down," and you're like, *yeah*. When the only thing that

makes you feel better is the idea of flattening someone
to the ground, then, yeah. Then you can tell me how
hard your fucking life is.

I didn't go right away. It's not like I dropped Isaac off
at home and then went straight over to the guy's house.
I told myself not to be an asshole. I remembered Ava and
what she said. She wasn't some prophet. People always
said about her that she was wise beyond her years. She
was a mental case. We both got fuck-up genes. The
fact that I stopped before I killed him just shows I'm at
least that much better than anyone expected of me. I
could have pummelled him. I could have mangled his
face right into his brains. Tangled it all with his long
black beard.

You seem like a good person. Young, even, with the
beard. Like that guy. When he was lying on the ground
crying at me, I was like, *Oh my God, he's probably not
much older than I am.* He has something like seven kids,
and I bet he's not even thirty. That's what Ava said to me
the last time we spoke. She said, "He's not even going
to be able to support his family now."

I know that. I didn't care then. I was so out of it,
I wasn't thinking of all the links. When I knocked
on his door and he came out of the house, I saw the
seven kids behind him. He was smart enough to close
the front door so that they didn't see anything. He
must have known why I was there. Or at least he got
it by the sound of my fist pounding against his door

frame. He lives in one of those townhouses where all the frummies and their extra-large families hang out. Those houses look like they're going to collapse in the next windstorm. When I banged on the door, bits of blue paint fell off like dried skin.

He said to me, "I'm very sorry. I really didn't see her."

I said, "You were talking on your fucking phone!"

He said, "No. I'm sorry. She walked in front of my car. She was talking on her phone. I couldn't stop."

Yeah. I couldn't stop either. Anger burned blue all the way through my veins, right into my fingers. Aching like when I was clutching that shovel. I went for his nose because the blood would come gushing out of his nostrils and I wanted it painted all over his starched white shirt. I wanted him to see what it was like for his blood to be splattered across the pavement. Maybe even so bad it came out of his ears. It's not like she asked for that, my grandmother. To have her blood painted all over the bakery parking lot like spilled evidence. There's something in your Torah about an eye for an eye, right? I think even God understands about revenge.

I mean, my sister's a soldier. She's gone off to protect the Jewish people. If they get bombed, they bomb right back. It's not personal; it's just the way it is. You have to look out for your people. You have to believe in something strongly enough that you're willing to put yourself on the line. I get it. There was nothing left in our family for her to believe in, so she had to go somewhere else. But then it's just me. I'm like the last man standing.

I couldn't just leave things the way they were, because otherwise no one would remember my grandmother. And now, whenever that guy looks in the mirror at his scars, he will think of her. His scars can be her scars, living on. Ava serving in her army, fighting for some ancient right handed down by God. She's so busy following orders, she probably doesn't remember how to think for herself. And even if she could, I bet she doesn't give five minutes a day to remembering our grandmother. Ava's not like that. She's always about moving forward.

But maybe you could reach her. Send her an email. Maybe she would listen if it came from you. I'd appreciate that, you trying. If you could tell her I'm doing a lot of thinking, then maybe she'll understand.

The Happiest Man on
Sunset Strip

AVA NEVER WANTED TO COME HOME. Right now, she is supposed to be getting her hair done with a bunch of the girls and telling Shira that she looks stunning on her wedding day. But instead, Ava's wrestling her great-uncle's wheelchair into the back of her rented sedan. He's sitting in the front passenger seat, snapping, "Faster!" Behind them is his care home, where Ava couldn't breathe. The whole place smelled like piss, except for Isaac's room, which smelled like shit because he shared it with a man who had been lying in a soiled diaper for hours. When Ava tried to open the window, which was on Isaac's side of the room, it wouldn't budge. He said, "They're afraid we'll escape. And there's the train tracks behind. Someone could get hurt."

Ava tugged upward anyway, but it was no use. She said, "No one here could climb out a window."

He said, "Until one day."

And Ava could see right then how he spent his days imagining an open window, an agile body, the grace of an acrobat or dancer, barely touching the ground as he slipped his way beneath the panes, somersaulted onto the bushes below, twisting and bending until every part of him was out of the building and he could see his still, empty bed from the freedom of the front lawn, the way the image of the bed disappeared as he backed away from the building. And then the farther he got, the more he would just see the reflection of the grass, bushes and sky in the glass, until it's as if his room didn't exist on the other side at all.

She'd taken him outside in his wheelchair and they were only going to visit for a few minutes in the courtyard. The hairdresser wasn't far from the home. Ava told the girls, "I just need to see my uncle. I'll meet you there." Isaac sat with his head tilted to one side, his eyes squinting against the high sun. Ava said then, "The girls are expecting me."

The left side of Isaac's face hung lopsided because of the stroke. He could speak, but he slurred his words, as if his tongue were swollen and heavy. He said, "This is the first time I've been outside since moving here." *This* became *dish. Firsht. He-yah.*

Ava said, "You tell me when you're ready to go back inside."

Isaac opened one eye. "I'm not."

ISAAC WANTS MCDONALD'S. He's craving salt. Ava has figured out the folding wheelchair. She's closed the car door and she's driving out of the parking lot with her great-uncle beside her, his head leaning against the window, and he's saying, "Fries. Not mashed potatoes."

"Do I have to have you back by a certain time?" Ava asks him. She hasn't seen him in seven years. She was only going to visit for half an hour at the most. She'd brought him some postcards from Israel that he could put up somewhere in his room. One of the Western Wall with the gold Dome of the Rock in the background. Another of the Dead Sea and someone floating on his back in the black water, reading a paper. In another life, Isaac had lived on a kibbutz, ate in a communal dining hall for every meal, got filthy working in the fields, attending to sunflowers. Ava didn't know him then, but she remembers his stories.

"Mud in my ears," he would say. "How does one get mud in their ears?"

She'd picked out the postcards at the airport, and they were still in her purse. She had thought she would put them up on his windowsill just before she left, so when he looked outside he could picture those places.

"Cheeseburger," he says. Isaac holds his left arm over his lap as if it were not attached to his body. His hand and fingers are puffy. With his right hand, he points at the drive-thru on the other side of the street where Ava will have to make a left turn.

"That's it," he says.

"Isaac," she says as she pulls up to the intercom, "I'm taking you back right after this."

"Large fries," he says. "Please."

AVA'S MOTHER, CARLY, had a habit of coming and going. Carly would say to her mother, Elaine, "If you don't take the kids, I'm going to have to call Child and Family." Ava's grandmother would say the same thing, "Carly, if you don't smarten up, I'll have to call Child and Family." Ava often felt like she was dangling by the end of this string called Child and Family and that one day either her mother or her grandmother was going to cut it with a pair of scissors.

The last time Carly left, she told Ava, "I'm good with hair. I always do yours, right? In Vegas, there are shows where people like me can show off our stuff, right? And someone will hire me from there. And then I'll send you and Adam plane tickets and you'll come too."

"Make me a French braid," Ava said. Carly sat on the bed on her knees and tugged at Ava's greasy hair. Carly said, "It's better like this. A little dirty. It will hold."

The braid held for a week after Carly left. Finally, Elaine yelled that Ava had to take it out or else she would cut it off. Ava sat on the toilet and screamed while her grandmother cut the braid with kitchen shears. Afterwards, Elaine sat on the floor of the bathroom and cried too. She clutched the braid, which looked like a squirrel's tail. Ava stopped screaming once it was done, but she stared at her grandmother. The yelping gave her the same kind of headache she got when she impatiently bit into a Popsicle. She felt the same kind of panic at not being able to make it stop.

THEY SIT IN THE McDonald's parking lot. Isaac asks Ava to rip the french fries in half so that he won't choke. He has the use of his right hand, but right now he needs to hold the armrest to keep himself upright. He says to her, "You have to feed me."

"I should take you back," she says.

"Just one. For the salt. There's no salt there."

Ava remembers her grandmother feeding her grandfather like this, the way he would stick his tongue out like a baby bird. She holds up half of a fry but looks away when Isaac leans forward to take it with his lips. They are dry and they scratch her fingers. She feels the tip of his tongue as he pulls the fry from her grasp. She's not sure why, but she thinks of the goldfish pond in the courtyard, of sticking her hand into the water and feeling the fish swim by her fingers, the scales rubbing across her fingertips.

"Another," he says.

"Isaac, let's go."

"One more. And the cheeseburger."

Ava's fingers shine with grease. After the army, she decided to stay in Israel. Now she works for an event planner who caters to families from North America who want to celebrate their children's bar or bat mitzvahs somewhere holy. She deals with religious people all the time, caterers, rabbis — her favourite florist covers her hair with three different scarves, wrapped in an enormous beehive, held in place by rhinestone brooches. Over there, Ava keeps kosher by accident. She has not torn at a cheeseburger in years. Even when she is out in Tel Aviv with friends, even when the meat is *treif*, she won't have the cheese. Though now, as she feeds bite-size pieces to Isaac, she wonders who she is kidding and why it even matters.

Isaac says, "You speak to your brother?"

"No."

"At least write him."

"I don't need the headache, Isaac. Don't lecture me."

"We don't choose our family," Isaac says. "You, me, him. That's all."

"What am I supposed to say to him? You know what he did to that man."

"I know."

Ava feeds him more burger. He sighs each time after he swallows. He chews the meat slowly, and he rolls the bread around in his mouth with his tongue. Ava hasn't had any of her fries yet, or her chicken nuggets. They've already grown cold.

"I didn't want to come back," Ava says. "Listen to all his excuses about how we had such a messed-up childhood. He thinks I left him. You know he'll say that, right? He'll find a way to blame me because I left him to make aliyah, and Bubby died and he had no one. I'm not his therapist, Isaac. If he screwed up his life, that has nothing to do with me."

"How much longer does he have?"

"Five years? I'm not coming back when he gets out. I'm not throwing him some welcome home party."

Isaac points at the milkshake and Ava lifts it to his mouth. She feels him tug on the straw. It reminds her of a calf she saw once, nursing. Tugging and tugging at the teat, though the mother stood still as if she couldn't feel a thing. Ava was visiting a farm on a school trip. She was little. The cow's tail swung like a metronome on top of a piano, like a time clock counting down until the calf's turn was up. Only there was no ending; the calf kept drinking and the tail kept swinging, and it never got down to zero.

Isaac takes long sips of his milkshake and Ava asks, "You want to drive some more?"

NEITHER OF THEM HAS thought this through. Ava takes Isaac back to her hotel. She wheels him up to her room, which has a queen-sized bed, a flat-screen TV. Isaac asks if he can watch golf. Ava sits him up in the bed with pillows behind his head and under his right elbow to keep him propped up. She takes off his white runners. The soles are not worn at all because he has never walked in them. But his socks have holes in the heels, both of them. Ava starts to make a list of things she will have to buy him before leaving for Israel in a few days. Socks. A small salt shaker. Does he need underwear?

"Take me to the washroom," he says to her. "The meat and my stomach."

"Isaac, I . . ."

"Just bring me there. You'll hold me while I sit."

"We should just go back," she says. Ava calculates how fast she can get him home. Fifteen minutes if he co-operates. She won't stop at the Walmart. She can stop by once more on her way to the airport, when she knows she has a hard stop, not a day so open-ended that she feels like her life and his are spilling out in all directions.

"Now," he says. He's leaning up and over the bed. She has to catch him under his arms; otherwise he will fall. He puts his right arm around her shoulders and drags his left foot behind as she walks him the five feet from the bed to the bathroom.

"Help me pull them down," he tells her. He can grab the right side of his pants, but not the left. His face is very close to hers because she's still propping him up. His breath smells off—sour like old whiskey, though they haven't been drinking. She turns her face away from his to cough and he says, "I need you now."

"Isaac, I can't do this," she says, but he's already shifting his pants over his bum, the elastic waist falling easily over his hips.

"You have to. Otherwise you'll be wiping me like a baby."

"This was a stupid idea," she says, but she gets his pants down around his knees. The whole time she's looking over his shoulder so that she doesn't have to see his penis.

"Lower me down."

She gets him so that he's sitting on the toilet, and then she tries to back away out of the bathroom. It's been newly renovated, sleek granite counter, a grey and blue shiny tile backsplash on the wall. There's a daylight bulb for putting on makeup, and Ava had switched it on by accident when they came stumbling in. Now she switches it off because it makes everything too bright in here. Illuminated.

"You finish up and I'm taking you back," Ava tells him. "I didn't come here to look after you."

He's shitting his lunch out, the treat that didn't agree with him. He's making noises like foghorns rattling in a chamber. He's grunting while his bowels let everything go. This all goes on for so long that Ava wonders what could possibly be left of him when he's done.

"You've forgotten," he says finally, after a deep breath. Ava is standing with her back to the bathroom door, which is open. She smells his diarrhea, the sharpness of it that then dissipates. She imagines the scent floating through the air like a siren; it comes out screaming at first and then becomes a whisper in the background as she gets used to the smell, which happens sooner than she expects.

"I'm only here because of you," he tells her. "You know that? Your grandmother begged me. I could be in California right now. She never told you that I came to help look after you guys?"

"I don't owe you anything."

When Ava is in Israel, there is so much about her old life she just doesn't think about. She calls Isaac from time to time. Once she heard a yelp in the background, like someone calling out in their sleep. Isaac said, "My roommate can't control himself. But it's just noise."

When she hung up then, she thought what a shame it was her uncle had to live like that. But that was it. She definitely never imagined she would be waiting outside a bathroom to help him wipe his ass. She had packed away the thought of Isaac with everything else—her incarcerated brother, her dead grandmother, her mother who never ever came back. No matter the promise. The great disappearing mama.

Ava leans against the wall beside the bathroom door.

"Get in here," Isaac says. "I can't get up."

"For God's sake, Isaac. At least say 'please.'"

"I'm not going to beg you!" he growls. She's never heard him really angry. He's an old dog, drooling out of the side of his mouth.

"Your mother was a spoiled brat," he says. "You've grown just like her."

Ava walks into the bathroom. She grabs toilet paper from the wall and rolls it around and around her hand. She holds her breath while she leans forward so that his forehead rests against her shoulder, and she reaches down to wipe him from behind. Ava has never wiped a baby, let alone an old man. She keeps her mouth closed to stop herself from gagging, but she's also biting her lip because she wants to cry looking at his flat bottom, the white hair growing in tufts from out of his crack and around his tailbone. This is everything she was afraid of about coming back.

He says, "You're no different to me than one of the nurses. There's even one that sort of looks like you. But she smiles more than you ever did."

Ava flushes the toilet. "You don't know any more about my mother than I do."

He puts his good arm around her back and says, "Stand me up so you can lift up my pants."

She does and she hears his knees crack. She feels his weight on her shoulders, the heaviness of his body as he lets out a long breath while she tries to pull upward on his underwear and pants. She thinks of an eighties movie she watched once with a man who worked in a department store dressing mannequins. One came alive. And of course he fell in love. And she was beautiful. He would carry her around and dress her in all kinds of outfits until he found the perfect one. It was something about how he controlled this statue until she

came to life and freed him from whatever was holding
him back.

Isaac knocks the lid closed, sits back down on the
toilet, and pats Ava on the back. He leans against the
wall and the counter by the sink with his eyes closed.
Ava sits on the floor and leans against the tub. She
thinks that he may have fallen asleep from all the activ-
ity; his mouth is partly open. But then he closes it and
swallows slowly and says, "Of course I do. She came
out to see me after she left here. She was a mess. I told
her to go back and be with her kids. And then I never
saw her again."

"What do you mean she came out to see you?"

Isaac opens his eyes now and Ava notices how they
droop, sacks of skin hanging in misshapen U's. She
doesn't remember him looking this way when she was
younger—perpetually sad.

Your grandmother knew she was coming my way.
She called me. She said, 'If Carly comes to you, don't
you help her. She needs to come back and be with her
kids.' And I said to her, 'If she's so messed-up, maybe she
shouldn't be with those kids.' But your grandmother
was always about getting Carly to do the right thing.
For you guys. You know, the kids would make her
straight. I saw all kinds of messed-up people in L.A.
who had kids and they didn't do shit for them.

"Carly showed up at my place. Shaking. Eyes all red.
She wanted a job or to sleep on my floor. I told her,

'You've got to be kidding. I'm not going to let you bring any of that shit into my life.'"

"What shit?"

"She was on all kinds of stuff. A walking chemical lab. Always was. Very experimental. You know that. Everyone knew that about her."

Ava doesn't answer. She doesn't say, *I don't know a fucking thing*. Even though she feels like she's been flipping channels all her life and finally she has stumbled on the show featuring her story.

Isaac says, "I let her come in. I gave her a cup of coffee. I had a good business, you know. I sold stuff on eBay. But I didn't need staff. And I told her that. I said, 'I don't need anyone to help me.' And she said something about all her stuff getting stolen on her way out there. She couldn't cut hair without her supplies. She wouldn't be any trouble. Sleep on the couch. She said, 'Isaac, you're my only hope.'

"I looked at her and I was like, 'You left your only hope back in Toronto.' But she was a wreck. So then I said, 'You must think I'm a real fool. You think I'm going to let you and your junkie friends shoot up around my place? What, you think I owe you? I don't owe you.'

"She said, 'You and me, we're the same, you know.' And I said, 'Nah. Nah, we're not.' And she said, 'Yeah. You just think you've got it all figured out. See, I know I don't. You just don't know it yet.'

"That made me mad, right? I never needed anyone. I never got married, right? I never had kids. And I was happy, right? I loved L.A. I loved the sun. I loved a good place to eat. I'd go out and people thought I was Dustin Hoffman. You know that? People used to come up to me with their script ideas. I signed some autographs. I lived in this place where everyone was trying to be someone, except for me. I was the happiest man on the Sunset Strip. Who the hell did she think she was?

"And if she hadn't been standing in front of me like that, shaking and stinking and looking at me like I was the one who didn't know what he was doing with his life, I might have taken her for dinner. I might have spent one evening with her. Maybe if she said she needed one night and then a lift to the bus station so she could make her way back home. You know, you didn't do anything to deserve her. And Elaine left all alone to raise you guys.

"I gave her a bunch of money. I don't remember, five hundred dollars? It was enough to get her back home. I gave it to her, she didn't ask. But I gave it to her and I said, 'This is enough to get you home. And you're going to take this to buy yourself a ticket.' But she knew she wasn't going to do that. And I knew she wasn't going to do that. It's not like I was giving her the money so that she could go get high. I just wanted her to leave. I said to her, 'This is all you're ever going to get from me.' And then she left.

"I didn't even tell Elaine that I saw her. You know that? When Elaine called and asked me to come back here to help her out with you guys, I never said a word. And I guess she never came back, eh? I guess that was it."

Ava doesn't think she has the strength to stand. She almost asks Isaac to help her up. Her mouth is dry and pasty. When she swallows, she feels like the back of her throat is sticking together.

"I probably would have done the same as you," she finally manages, as if they weren't talking about her mother but some stranger who needed kindness for one night. As if, after all this time, there wasn't any difference. "I'm not going to blame you." But even as she says this, she knows she won't ever come back. She can't possibly do any of this again.

He says, "You need to get me home."

WHEN AVA WHEELS ISAAC from the car back to the home, he says to her, "I didn't mean it. You're not like your mother. You're kinder. You're not nearly as selfish."

"She had her demons," Ava says. It's a line her grandmother used to use. *Carly's demons*, like the way some kids collected stuffed animals, or stickers. Ava used to imagine her mother lining up her demons on a shelf, dusting them. Shining their little heads, because in Ava's imagination they were made out of pewter.

"You're more together than she was. Way more. People must say you're doing pretty well. Considering."

"People don't know," Ava says. She pushes the wheelchair across the front mat. The electronic door to the home slides open. She's hit with the smells of ammonia and chlorine, and then fish sticks because it's now suppertime and they are passing right by the dining room. A nurse walks over from behind the front counter.

"Isaac! We didn't know where you were. And you almost missed supper. Did your daughter take you for something to eat?"

The nurse comes around the back to take over pushing the chair and Ava lets her. Ava backs away toward the sliding doors, like she has to get there before they close and lock her in. She says, "Okay. Bye, Isaac. Take care."

The nurse turns the chair around and Isaac is waving at her with his good hand. He's calling, "Really! I meant it. You're so much better."

But Ava is already running out the doors, stumbling into the outside, spitting out her breath like she ate something she couldn't stand. She's digging through her purse to find some tissue for her running nose, for the saliva around her mouth. She pulls out the postcards that she never gave Isaac and she folds them into quarters, rips them into squares and then tosses them into the garbage, all those pieces of sunshine and prayer and golden, gleaming sand.

ACKNOWLEDGEMENTS

Writing may be a solitary act, but I learned so much about the importance of community while working on this book. Thank you to:

Everyone at the Sarah Selecky Writing School. To my teachers, Jennifer Manuel and Lana Pesch, for pushing me to dig deeper with my stories. To my fellow students, for your encouragement and wise critique. To my fellow faculty, for including me in your writing life. To Nicole, for the Friday emails. To Sarah, for believing in me, cheering me on, and celebrating every step.

To Jami Attenberg and the Humber School for Writers for the space, guidance, and accountability to pen the first draft of this collection.

To Zsuzsi Gartner and Jennifer Manuel for your early evaluations of this manuscript.

To Marnie Ferguson for the phone calls, laughs, and pep talks.

To the incredible team at House of Anansi Press. Maria Golikova, managing editor; Jennifer Lum and the design team for the gorgeous cover; Linda Pruessen for your great copyediting eye, Sue Sumeraj for your expert proofreading; everyone in marketing and sales for championing this book, especially Laura Chapnick and Curtis Samuel. Many thanks to Sarah MacLachlan and Janie Yoon for enthusiastically bringing this collection on board. Janie, thank you for always being there. Most of all, thank you to Michelle MacAleese, my brilliant editor and friend, for all your guidance and support.

To my VCFA community, for all the love and for inspiring me daily to pick up my pen.

To my family: my parents, my siblings, and my in-laws, for always celebrating my ups and never letting me get stuck in my downs.

To my kids: Boaz, Dalya, and Isaac, for reminding me to keep going, even when it's hard.

And especially, to Jason, who never let me stop, keeps me on track, and has always believed this dream of mine would become a reality. I love you for all this and so much more.

Author photograph: Katherine Fogler Photography

SIDURA LUDWIG is the author of the novel *Holding My Breath*, which was shortlisted for the Carol Shields Winnipeg Book Award. Her short fiction has been published by numerous literary journals and anthologies. She works as a communications specialist and creative writing teacher, and her creative nonfiction has appeared in several newspapers and on CBC Radio. She is currently working on her M.F.A. in Writing for Children and Young Adults through the Vermont College of Fine Arts. Originally from Winnipeg, Manitoba, she now lives in Thornhill, Ontario, with her husband and their three children.